In the Air

Johns Hopkins: Poetry and Fiction
John T. Irwin, General Editor

ROBERT NICHOLS

In the Air

The Johns Hopkins University Press
Baltimore and London

This book has been brought to publication with the generous assistance of the G. Harry Pouder Fund.

© 1991 The Johns Hopkins University Press
All rights reserved
Printed in the United States of America

The Johns Hopkins University Press
701 West 40th Street
Baltimore, Maryland 21211
The Johns Hopkins Press Ltd., London

Library of Congress Cataloging-in-Publication Data
Nichols, Robert, 1919–
    In the air / Robert Nichols.
        p.   cm. — (Johns Hopkins, poetry and fiction)
    ISBN 0-8018-4195-X. — ISBN 0-8018-4196-8 (pbk.)
    I. Title. II. Series.
PS3527.I323715 1991
813'.54--dc20   90-26164

Page 164 constitutes a continuation of the copyright page.

For Kerstin, Duncan, Eliza

■ Contents

■ O N E

The Changing
Beast

■ The Secret Radio Station

1

In our town there is a secret radio station.

"Why secret? Everyone knows about it. It's evangelical."

Its secret is that it is beamed only toward our town. (The station can't be located.) But it isn't heard anywhere else.

The secret is in its place, not in its message. Still, the message is given in an unknown language. Words, a vocabulary that we don't share. Therefore one can say what is broadcast is secret.

At the same time everyone knows what the message of the radio station is: simply a picture of the way the town was in the past and the way it can be.

Still, the language itself, the medium in which the message is sent out, is not understood. It's difficult to say how everyone knows the message. And there are some that deny this really is the message. It could be a commercial message of some kind, one just designed to sell products. There are intervals, definite breaks in the continuous flow of the unknown language—this could be commercials. Though of course we can't be sure of it.

Anyway it's only the music that people listen to. This is folk rock—or "Jesus rock"—in a completely familiar style.

As I say, the location of the radio station, that is, the broadcasting studio and transmitter, is not known. Therefore, though the broadcast comes to us every day, it is distrusted.

Still, it's natural to regard this as our station. It's number 98.5 on the dial. A convenient spot, right in the middle of the dial. And this may be another reason the station is so popular. When it was first started there were attempts to find out where the broadcasting was originating, that is, its source. But this is no longer considered important.

The town is divided. There are those who believe in the message. And the skeptics who say that the message is only commercials. But this couldn't be true, because the commercials come only at intervals. It makes sense that the message is about the town, since it's only beamed at the town and nowhere else. It's true the songs are the most popular, but the rest of the program must be about the town. It must have something exclusively to do with the town business, the affairs of the town, personalities. It would be different if it were heard anywhere else in the United States. It would be a national language understood by everyone, wherever it was broadcast. Like other evangelical stations. But this is only heard by us; therefore it must be about us.

Part of its attraction, to skeptics and believers alike, may be that the language *is* foreign. Since you're listening to the music and you're turning off the words mentally, an effort is involved, more energy is required. It's never dull or repetitive. In this sense the station is more challenging than other stations (what we're beginning to think of as the "national" stations).

So in spite of everything, this is the one most listened to. There is what you might call a willful suspension of disbelief.

It is conceivable that the language of the radio station could be translated. I doubt if it would be a difficult project of linguistics which could only be done by some professor—like the Rosetta Stone. That was a dead language; it existed only in a fragment. There were no known speakers—whereas we listen to our own evangelical station every day. There are patterns, elements of form, like any other radio station. These don't need to be deciphered at all. It's like watching the television screen with the sound off. (In fact, it's exactly the reverse of that.) What is happening on the screen, what the figures are—a family around the kitchen table making jokes, a cowboy riding across the desert—who is doing what, is all perfectly comprehensible. Though it looks a little dumb, as though a joke were being played on the actors.

Regarded in that light, our own broadcast might strike someone as comical or banal. There are the intervals of the commercials. Each song is followed by some kind of announcement or explanation. Then there are long passages that are very *heartfelt*. This must be the evangelical message. These are passages which can only be described as *sincere*. It might be possible to take something that is absolutely known—like the weather. I don't mean the weather is known beforehand. But after it's happened it's a matter of facts and figures. It's conceivable—probably not even difficult to do—that these might be correlated with recordings of the radio station over a long period of time. One could assume that a certain block of time, certain programmed spots throughout the day, would be for the weather. This would have a repetitive pattern; certain sounds and phrases would be repeated. These would be keyed into the actual weather data. This could yield other connections, etc., so that finally one would understand the whole language.

But this might possibly be disappointing. And in any case it wouldn't make that much difference, since we know the message anyway—at least the logic of the message. One can imagine every town in the whole country having something like that. Maybe not in the early days of radio when its attraction, the significance of it, was national, but particularly now when local programming is fairly popular. To us anyway this language has become more and more familiar simply as it becomes an accompaniment to what we do every day, the rhythm of things, what all of us do, though not what anyone does individually—the particular rhythm of the town. So that we know it anyway, but on an intimate and deep level below consciousness.

So it possibly is our natural language. And we have just forgotten it.

2

We were in the barber shop. A man was tipped back in the chair, a white lava on his face. The barber was working over him. Big front window. The main street outside: A & P store, post office, and gas station. A man came in, leaving his wife and kids outside in a beat-up Chevy, and began talking to us in a loud, bragging voice. We were sitting on the row of chairs by the window.

This was Alvin Basswood. We had all seen him at town meeting. During the rest of the year you wouldn't hardly see Alvin. He stuck to the back roads. That's not to say if you met up with him on the road, and happened to stop, he wouldn't roll down the car window and talk to you. Or if you met up with him at the post office (the motor of the Chevy running, whole family or some neighbors packed in the back as always). I mean that on the day of town meeting Alvin put on a performance, a spectacle— hobbling down the center aisle of the auditorium with his cane and saying he was a war veteran and had been gassed with agent orange, his credentials for speaking to the nation. They used to say: if you were on one side of a proposal and Alvin was against you, you'd win. So now, when he came into the steaming barber shop, there he was.

"'Lo Alvin."

"How you doing, Alvin?"

"Morning, Alvin. How are things down in your neck of the woods?"

In addition to being the town spectacle, Alvin was both fasci-nating and boring to talk to. He was off the wall mostly, but at the same time he was smart in a pedantic kind of way, always quoting facts and figures, waving some government report out of the car window at you. Wavy brown hair and white puffy face— probably from being sedentary in the car all day (with the rest of them all jammed in there in the back seat and not saying any-thing).

Beside this he was also the chief of the Mohawk Indians in the town. You knew there were Mohawk Indians in general. But it was always a surprise they were here specifically, actually living in town. Not all of them in the woods either. Not all of them had the worst jobs, though most of them were poor.

There was a radio sitting on the shelf where all the bottles of aftershave lotion were, tuned to station 98.5.

We had been sitting quietly, some of us reading the newspaper, listening to the chopping of the shears. Maybe absorbing the smell of Wildroot. I suppose that had made us sleepy . . . before Alvin came in.

Suddenly he stopped talking. It was as if he picked up his ears. Stood there leaning on his cane, listening to the radio. It got all his attention.

"You're not going to believe this . . . I'm in the process of making inquiries . . . " He was talking loudly, a look came into his eyes.

I figured at that moment he was going to tell us the secret of the language. That maybe he knew it, it was Mohawk. And besides he knew exactly where the broadcasting station was and had even been there. Maybe even from the time of the original search party. Or he'd found out about it later, during his travels up the back roads.

But then he switched to something else. He was telling us about a lawsuit—he called it a "legal action"—about a septic tank. It was against one of the neighbors, or against the selectmen, I couldn't tell which. I knew he was going to go running on about his complaint.

That moment of expected revelation had passed.

3

You and I have often been out walking in the woods. And of course in our part of the country there haven't always been woods. Time has reclaimed the land from the farmers.

Let us follow one of these stone walls. It will lead us nowhere. We can follow it for miles through the deep woods, a barely visible line running from one tree trunk to another, steeped in shade. Pine needles. Beech leaves. Clumps of fern. At right angles another wall will come in. The wall itself somewhat disheveled. In places actually buried. Solidly piled rock loosened, weakened by a century of frost heaves . . . has actually lost weight.

In the same way, the language changed over time. Certain phrases altered. Emptied of meaning . . . words hollowed out from the inside.

Not that what we're saying is false. The language doesn't lie. There's just a displacement. A jar where you come up against a different reality. . . though the words are the same.

Following a stone wall is like following a language.

All day through the deep woods, following the same route as the farmer did with his oxen and stoneboat, sweating in the sun.

4

Sheila is our town clerk. A smart woman but underpaid. But all town clerks are underpaid. And they're mostly smarter than other people. "A high level of technical competence" is the phrase used. Our Sheila puts out the town report, all eighty-odd pages, and takes it down to the printer's. Handles investments—money market account is the term used—besides the day-to-day business of filing, of licensing, and the twice-yearly business of dog rabies shots.

You will recognize in this a true portrait.

I always enjoy going into the town clerk's office—if I have some business that gives me an excuse. It takes the excuse of business to see Sheila. Always unnervingly busy. Everything done on time . . . at its time. The smallest thing, the largest. Otherwise it wouldn't get done. Always extraordinarily busy. But serene, self-possessed. Cool. I'm standing at the desk in muddy overshoes. Sheila is on the other side. On the phone . . . maybe town business or talking to the children at home. Scratch pad in front of her. A frown of concentration. Something on the paper . . . squinting slightly. I think this frown—reluctance to look up—is lovely.

I dreamed I brought her a rose.

In the back of the town clerk's office there is a musty, cramped, dimly lit area for ancient files. Property deeds. Like a crypt. Our town offices are next to the cemetery, and I always think of this part of it as part of the cemetery. Sometimes Sheila enters into this storage depot of ghosts. I wonder, will she come out again? First she pulls on a sweater (it's cold). Stands at the top step with her note pad. Pushing back her hair, and frowning, she disappears into the past.

In front and to the left as you go into the town hall is the Listers' office. Property is evaluated here. Constant real estate transfer. Fair Market Value, everything is based on. The listers themselves are two old dairy farmers whose farms themselves were sold. And now expedite the process.

The town hall itself (at the back is the clerk's office) is large.

"Ample" is the word used. "Roomy" is the word used. Here zoning board meetings are held. Board of Selectmen meets. Voting booths are set up on election day. A ceremonial space mostly empty, colder than the rest of the building and gloomy.

In my dream, I walk through this room toward the office and Sheila, holding a rose. Acute sense of embarrassment. Meeting is being held. All of them farmers. They have enormous square beards and square hats. It's the year 1840. They've just voted to build a schoolhouse on a spot convenient to the other farmsteads. And for salary of the schoolteacher, each farmer is to contribute two bushels of corn.

I go through and find in the back office Sheila broadcasting this meeting over the radio.

She is covered with confusion as I come in, mortified at being discovered.

5

A team of experts has arrived to find the hidden radio station. They have been given a map of the township by Sheila. Alvin Basswood has taken them through the back roads pointing out the possible sites. But knowing Alvin, we don't know whether this had helped them or confused them. Of course, they are loaded down with state-of-the-art technical equipment, tracking devices, airwave modulators, frequency detectors. But once within the town borders, they have been disoriented. The team has got lost in the woods. And once stuck in the mud of a logging road so that Huggett's tow truck had to be called to pull them out.

The reason they have come is that the station is unlicensed. As to the fact that it broadcasts in an unknown language, this doesn't concern them in the least. Nor the fact that the potential revenue to the Federal Communications Agency from such a tiny operation (we are talking about a twenty-square-mile area) would be insignificant. There is some higher principle involved. Also there may have been a tip-off by an informer. The station may have been reported by elements in the town hostile to it.

There are people in the town—I've heard some of them at the

barber shop—who don't like evangelism. It may have been the barber himself. (The ones standing most in need of prayer are against it.) The difficulty of being successful evangelically, that is, of converting anybody through an unknown language, seems to have escaped the barber. On the other hand, it may be that the unknown quality of the language, its complete unintelligibility, may be a help to conversion.

In any case the search party has made no progress. Once one gets off the main road, especially the secondary roads, one can easily get lost. Because the land is dense forest, gullies, and rock caves where there may be foxes and coy-dogs. For the search party to keep their bearings, they would have to pay attention to the markings and boundary lines, which are recorded on the town map. Without knowing these, even if they found the radio station, they wouldn't know where they were. The station could possibly be located from the air, on an aerial survey, but not on the ground. The only way the team can get anywhere is when they are accompanied by the listers. Who are of course able to follow the stone walls and are able to make sense of them because they know where the boundaries of the original fields are. This from a time when the whole countryside was open and therefore quite simple.

In addition to the array of technical and electronic experts, there is a team of translators trying to figure out the broadcasts, to decipher the language.

But in all the months they have been working on it, they've been able to translate only a single word: TOWN.

6

While I was in the Second World War I was on an island in the Pacific. Somewhere off the coast of Dutch New Guinea. A small island where the crabs would come out of the water in the moonlight and cover the beach like a kind of shimmering skin.

We were across from the harbor. A lone Japanese plane would fly in low over the headland and try to get near the ships, only to be caught in a fireworks display.

In twenty seconds it was over. Then we would lie in our fox-
hole looking up at the night sky. This hole was the length and
width of our cots—which were along beside us in the tent, with
our clothes on a hanger, our footlocker, and bundles of letters,
articles of home.

It was beautiful, with this excuse to be awake, lying on my
back in the earth under the tropic sky. But needless to say, we
were lonely. There all of us would listen to a program on the
Japanese radio: Tokyo Rose. She talked intimately to us, joked
with us, played us the latest records. One of them I remember
was Bing Crosby's "White Christmas."

This was the Japanese radio, but since it was our language, it
was playing the top song hits, giving us information and what we
knew of the news. You could say it was our national radio.

Tokyo Rose. She knew the regiments and companies . . . even
some of the men by name. I would try to picture her. Some girl
from Brooklyn, spiteful against the United States.

In the middle of the war, we lay there in the earth listening to
Tokyo Rose speaking to us in our own language. How old was
she? What did she look like? Did she have a figure? Blonde or
brunette?

I used to think of her as betraying me, as a traitor.

But now I think my own language is the traitor.

■ The Mirror of Narcissus

Under the spell of beauty. As we say, the beloved object bewitches us. Which one of us has not been in love sometime? The power, the authority of beauty. Her face and form, the way the hair falls like water over the neck, those blue eyes . . .

But in this case the beloved object is myself. This is the spell of Narcissus cast upon me. I am enchanted.

What is the cause, the agency of this? We say that Narcissus is enchanted by this reflection. The pool acts as a mirror as I bend down.

But what if the opposite happened? Instead of the reflection as I bend down, the surface opens. It does not reflect but opens up like the shutter of a camera. There is another person standing below looking up at me. This is the enchantment of the other. The circle of sky over my head, blue and framed by a few leaves, has become the blue of his world.

AN EXTREME CASE

I always like to think in extreme cases: and the patch of sky becomes an apartment building, say, in Calcutta. The beggar is squatting on the sidewalk looking up at the windows of the apartment house, a modern building, or at the entrance marquee. Perhaps diners are going into a restaurant inside. He is holding out his begging bowl. Brown skin, a soiled turban and loincloth that is no less foul and dirty. Emaciated limbs. We are looking into the large liquid eyes of the Indian, from which the light has almost gone out. As we look, it is extinguished in the pool.

I must tell you this comes from a memory—transformed into

an image. My wife and I were traveling in Chile. We were in Santiago. We had gone to the movies and had to stand in line for the next showing. A woman from the slums—called *poblaciones*—was sitting on the sidewalk with two small children. She was selling something from a flat box. Mangoes. The children played by the ticket window almost at our feet. I'm not sure it was mangoes. It may have been bunches of cornflowers she was selling, or straw flowers dipped in blue dye. One of them, the little girl, could barely walk, a toddler. The woman watched distractedly, at the same time narcotized. She seemed barely concerned with the children, or with selling the flowers either. As you know, this scene is repeated with variations for anyone who has traveled in these countries.

I didn't realize at the time that this was merely an example of what was then a prevailing economic condition. "Underemployment." I first came across the word in a Santiago newspaper. Unemployment, underemployment. As the black market is a hidden economy—it's there but not officially recognized—the world of underemployment is a hidden economy. That is, reality is hidden behind a veil.

Presumably we are talking about large quantities of people. The aggregate. At the same time we have to notice that the language, which is the language of economics/statistics deadens, numbs as with Novocaine, precisely *this story* of the individual.

The story of the woman and the children on the sidewalk is deemphasized and one could say it is of no interest. It doesn't tell how she got there, what was happening at home, what was in her mind when the decision was made, etc. For instance, I imagine it was in the barrio of Los Gatos, in a little house next to a machine shop. At the edge of the pasture . . . exceedingly dry at this time of year, a tawny brown color, becoming the foothills of the surrounding mountains. It's hard to tell from the outside whether these barrios are rich or poor. On the street a mangy dog picking over a pile of garbage—a sight one finds everywhere in Santiago. Of course, inside the house it's different. We might imagine a conversation between Maria and her sister. The husband is out, maybe at a bar drinking. We know he's not working. Or he could be at a political meeting. No sense in always looking at the pathetic, that is, the passive side. In any case there's no food in the house. And Maria says:

"I think I'll go down to El Centro. To the cinema."

The sister says nothing; she shrugs. It's a long trip to the Center by bus. Maria's children and some others from the neighborhood are in the yard. She'll take only the two youngest ones.

"I'm going to buy mangoes. These people like them."

"Do you have the money?"

A sharp question from the sister. It touches on everything, the woman's dress, the shelves, the pot of rice and beans on the stove. Her own house, which is down the street, is better.

"I can buy a few in the market when I get off the bus. And the man gives me a box. Carajo, the price of fruit nowadays even mangoes."

Where these women come from, the countryside, this was not a fancy fruit.

"How much are they, a box of mangoes?"

"30 pesos."

"You're taking a big risk. Tomorrow you could go without eating anything. And there's the carfare. You could buy food for tomorrow."

"Hey, if I sell mangoes every day I can put money in the bank. No, but I could stay ahead of the game at least. If I could sell the whole box of mangoes. You can do it in two hours. Sometimes a half hour. But some nights are long; you don't sell them."

No mention is made of the toll this will take on the children. They are already tired and cranky because they have not been fed. There'll be the long bus ride into town, the mother trying to control them squirming on the seat. Their faces are sallow, without color, the clothes dirty and ragged. No attempt—for this trip—to substitute something better. The sallowness of the children will be an advantage. Nor will she worry about herself. Ordinarily a trip to a public place—where one is to be seen . . . there would be a feeling of *shame*, she would wash their faces and dress them better. But this one is past that point long ago.

Maybe the sister has children in the yard, playing around the swing. She goes to the open door to look at them.

"Okay, I'll stay here. Maybe I'll be here when you get back. But don't count on it."

This is merely a notation. We can only sketch this scene in the imagination. *Therefore* it has no authority.

PRIVATE SPELLS / COLLECTIVE DELUSIONS

I would like to say at this point that I am interested in the fact of underemployment in Chile—and not interested. And *you* are both interested and not interested. What is happening in the economic condition of men in other countries is not a path that at the moment we want to follow. Or perhaps it is too much of a path; that road has been trodden too many times to tell us anything new.

In the story of Narcissus we think of the youth, or of the young woman bending down—and startling with surprised pleasure at her face. This is happening for the first time. This story is always new. There is something eternally innocent about this. As if she has not seen a reflection in the water before. Of course, there must always be this first time. We think of the young woman bending down. The novelty, the magic of the world caught upside down. She's thirsty. The coolness, deep shade. There is a stillness. A fresh smell of mint. In a circle behind her head, the sky is framed with leaves.

Why is it that, in art, in literature, images are organized around the individual? It is because the individual is *here* . . . listening. It is his or her consciousness that absorbs, takes in the impression; the individual is one who responds and feels, as if the image in a moment of desire *offers itself* to the individual consciousness. So much so that these characters I have been reading about, charged with this light and energy, stay with me when I close my eyes on the book. They are in the darkness with me. The story moves through my dreams.

Since we are talking about the Narcissus theme, what is necessary to explore now is how the image of Narcissus falling in love with himself in the pool—which is in itself private, solitary and somewhat shameful (most delusions are private—the intrusion by a stranger breaks the spell, exposes the hidden shame). When can it become a collective delusion? What is more interesting in our time is the collective delusion. It is in fact the pervasive experience of our time.

But Narcissus is about private delusion. It can't be about something else. Is it that there is no mirror large enough?

For instance (I'm taking a familiar example) a line of Americans stretching across the continent holding hands for hunger, for the starving in Africa. This is a collective delusion. On a colossal scale. It is Narcissus calling to Narcissus.

Why is it a collective delusion? It is a delusion because, at the same time as the national sentiments were building up—I mean of course sentiments of generosity, concern, open-handedness—at the same time the organized system was being developed (which one can only call a machine) of world trade, certain financial mechanisms, etc., the transfer of terms of goods/raw materials/food, etc. . . . Always the transaction involved a net loss to *them*—no matter what was happening, whatever the historical stages. In fact the current flowed the other way. The current of the heart flowed one way, the current of acquisition, the other. From the rest of the world significantly more was being extracted than was put back. The delusion was: that we were *giving* to them.

The system has become invisible in itself, like a mirror. As the surface of the water has become invisible in itself. One doesn't see what is going on behind it, only the reflection. The machine of economic transfer has become a silvered mirror. It reveals nothing.

HAWTHORNE'S PATIENCE

The writer Nathaniel Hawthorne and his two sisters are visiting the city of Florence, Italy, in the year 18—. They are staying at a small hotel or boarding house called the *Pensione Inglese*. In the dining room is heavy black walnut furniture in a provincial style, linen tablecloths, blue china, each table with a vase of flowers. As its name implies, the hotel caters to Englishmen and the rare American tourist of taste. The dining room is cool and dark, but with a door opening into the garden. At mealtimes acquaintances are made. The dining room is a hive of conversation, a nest of *intimacy* for a few weeks. The two sisters are intrigued by these stories of attachments, of obscure past histories, among the guests. Personalities are discussed, amorous possibilities (for instance that Miss B. of Philadelphia has fallen in love with a young British barrister and cricket player). Historic spots, trips into the countryside that one party or another are about to take. Hawthorne himself sits unresponsive with his eye on the garden door. What is out there?

A month has gone by. Hawthorne every day steals out into the garden from which a tower, *campanile*, can be seen through leaves. The garden has a high wall and is shaded by avocado and ilex trees. Worn statuary green with moss sunk into the shrubbery. The street noises of the town are far away, there are not even any birds.

At the edge of the pool he bends down, waiting for someone to appear, for something to happen.

Miss B. is wrestling with the coachman or with an Italian miller. It is a night rendezvous; she has gone to him after getting his sign. They are in a windmill. Outside is the landscape of Italy. Furiously she resists; her blouse is torn. They are both standing on the mill floor fifteen feet up from the ground as the windmill turns. The burly miller is trying to wrestle her against the wall, onto the floor. But she is resisting. Moral strength can't last forever. She will succumb finally, collapse in his arms, and he will take her standing up. Meanwhile both figures are sweating and groaning—it is extremely hot. Now more articles of her clothing are ripped off. Both figures are covered with flour.

These stories are the fantasies of the female and male guests at the Pension Inglese.

You will notice that in these fantasies the Italians are dream figures, the miller, the coachman—corresponding to erotic de-

sires. Beyond that, nothing of them is known. Whereas the fig-
ures of Miss B., the barrister, and others in the party of American
and English tourists are well known. In the dreamer, the figures
of the lover emanate from sexual desires, as the figures of hunger
emanate from the fear of hunger or the fascination with hunger.

The tourists are familiar. In the grammar of storytelling they
are authentic. They are real people; we recognize them because
we know them—even though the story may be trivial, even re-
pelling. We know these characters/personalities as well as we
know our own faces.

It is the others Hawthorne is standing by the pool waiting for.
The others who are strangers. But who are they? How will they
show themselves? That is why he is so patient. This is why he
slipped out the dining room door, why he has been coming again
and again to the pool.

THE DOUBLE BARRIER

In fact the writer, Hawthorne, confronts a double barrier. There
is the garden glade with its gravel paths, its unkempt shrub-
bery—in a *style* of abandonment, a wilderness in the midst of the
city. Still, the disturbing voices are close, coming from the dining
room of the hotel, a constant hubbub of voices—whose owners
he knows—each with a distinctive name. But this is a distrac-
tion. He is embarrassed, bored by these love affairs, every turn,
every nuance of which he knows. Meanwhile the country—
Italy—is eluding him.

He dislikes it that the audience of the play has become the
subject of the play. That the readers of his stories have become
the subjects of his stories.

Secondly (this is the second barrier) the writer of fictions can-
not write about large numbers. But what's this country—to
which he has traveled, where he wants to *be*, even though it is
foreign to him—what is it but large numbers of people all of
whom are foreign to him? He is interested in each one, he wants
to make stories of them. He is after their personalities, desires,
what they are in their deepest being. But the being itself dis-
solves into something wider, some deeper destiny in which they

become obscure. Some medium in which the individual is held in suspension. The story itself becomes a distorting factor. He is waiting patiently at the pool's edge. He is quiet, in readiness; his mind is concentrated, etc. for the figures that are to appear. But it is as if his presence, the very fact of his attention, keeps them from surfacing.

THE PERFECTION OF THE MACHINE

The system mystifies itself. The phrase is itself a mystification. We think of veils, covers, trails covered up and obscured. At each turning of the route a false trail, a false sign.

The veil of commodities.

There is no gift—even the gift of modernity—given in innocence. Without its price.

For instance in India when the first British textiles were brought in, in order to discourage/limit local competition, that is, weaving of the local cloth "kahdi," there was a law against handicrafts. A village weaver spinning and weaving kahdi was to have his hand cut off.

The language of the past names the things of the past.

On what was once his "milpa," the field on which the peasant grew his corn, the paddy where he grew rice, now he cuts cane, now he cuts jute, sisal fiber (for manilla rope).

The labor buys back his bread.

And in between crops, in the dead season, he starves or goes to the city. This demystifies the phrase: "the substitution of export-oriented goods for subsistence goods." But it is not the language of the system. Where there is no bowl of rice or corn taken away. Only cash is exchanged for jute and cane sugar.

What is significant about the cane cutter, his sweat, his eyebrows clogged, his skin prickly with the cane fibre—these qualities have been erased long ago.

The language of the past names only the things of the past. But the machine, that is the system, has absorbed history. The machine has its own language, the language of operation. Behind its bright reflecting surface everything else is concealed, it is forgotten. It lies deep down, a sediment at the bottom of the pool.

MASKS / GESTURES

The long line of Americans stretching across the continent are seeing only the gesture of hunger, the mask. And each is wearing his own mask.

MARIA AGAIN

One would think that for the writer—even with a minimum of means, of talent—in order to penetrate the pool, to plumb its depths below the surface, all that is necessary is to stretch out one's hand. To shatter what is merely an image, a reflection, could not be an act of violence.

But there remains the problem of authenticity. Am I able to write a story which is not mine?

I mentioned before (we were drawing a sketch of a Chilean woman selling flowers—I think it was flowers, or was it fruit or pencils? In front of the movie theater in downtown Santiago. It was at random. We focused on this figure rather than on so many others. The incident drawn from a personal memory while traveling) . . .

It was intriguing to imagine where she came from—the barrio of Los Gatos—or was it Mapuches? What were her intentions? / feelings? What did she go through to get here on that particular evening? etc.

Now: to get into it a little further . . .

We are back at the house in Los Gatos. Maria has been getting the children ready. She is saying to her sister (we will call her in this story "Jenny"),

"Jenny, you stay here. Alfredo will be back later—from El Centro." Maybe he was hanging around the park . . . maybe he's working there.

Or she says: "Jenny, did you see the kids' shoes? I gotta put shoes on them when we go down there. They'll be walking on the sidewalk, there's glass. It's not the same as the yard, where you can go barefoot. I'm not going to dress them." (She's referring to the two little ones. The doors and windows are open, the older children are playing outside on the swing.) "Somebody's got to watch them. You stay here. Maybe I'll see you when I get back."

Jenny: "Listen, I was on my feet all day. You come back and I'll be sleeping."

The sister is not helping find the shoes. She is looking at herself in the mirror.

"Do you like this eyeshadow? You don't think it's too much?"

"No, it's a nice color. It goes with the dress." (The sister has made over a dress or has bought a new one at the department store where she works.)

Possible Conversations:

(Little girl) "I'm hungry."

"I'll make you supper when we get home."

　　　* * *

"I'm hungry. I want that." (At the bus stop. The boy points to a candy bar in the store.)

"You can't have it. Later, you can have one. I don't want your face all smeared with chocolate when we're in there, trying to sell mangoes."

　　　* * *

(On the bus) "Peeto. Stay on the seat. I don't want you running all over the bus. Peeto, sit down by me. I'll smack you." (But the boy has slid from the seat, he's on the floor, people have to step over him. He's running up and down the aisle of the bus.) "You'll be sorry. I'm going to tell your father what you've been doing. And you better not be running around at the movie theater like that. What did I tell you, Peeto?"

"I gotta play on the sidewalk."

"You can play. But you can't go running around. There's a lot of people there watching. They're some bad people, they could grab you if you don't stay close to me. They could steal you and take you back to their home."

　　　* * *

(In El Centro. Little girl pulling at her arm)

"My feet are tired. Why don't you carry me?"

"How am I supposed to carry you? When I got this box?"

Obviously there are a number of stories, each one intriguing: the sister, the trip into downtown with two small children, the relation of the children to the father, etc. Where is the father? These stories would take us away from the main point: the need to put some food on the table, the need on the part of the woman to do something with what she has, to fend against hunger. It is not the others, it is this story that we want.

The *tone* of Maria's story is comic or sad. Comic depending on how many times she had done this before, whether she is an old hand . . . has taken up her stand there many evenings. It's her regular place, she's fought for it . . . other street sellers have other territories.

Or sad/pathetic/tragic: if it's the first time. She was at home with the children. There was nothing to eat. The idea came to her. Nobody she could leave them with. So she would have to take them with her.

One could almost say the possibilities are endless. As the people are endless. So many subjects, we needn't have chosen Maria. We are speaking of "underemployment," as this condition is called. There is an occupation/an employment which is never employment enough. An endless migration to the city, a community of the sidewalks.

No doubt Maria is thinking somewhat of this world—the world in which she is located—seeing it as she rides the bus into El Centro. Through the windows of the bus . . . the industrial suburbs, lots with weeds and chain link fences, as the riders speed by. All the cities of the world the same—Lagos, Rio. It is the magnet of hunger that is drawing them.

As the bus approaches El Centro the traffic is heavier. On the downtown streets the bus has already slowed down. Passengers are standing. Maria notes the driver has a kind of fringed red curtain above the windshield from which a doll is hanging. He is making change with one hand and driving with the other. She gets out at the final stop. It's the stop for the central market as well. Throngs of people. Friday night, everybody's shopping. Or maybe because it's nice weather. The market is a large building open at the sides. The aisles full of jostling seekers and buyers.

After struggling to get the children to the far end, she buys the mangoes from the man. He knows her. A campanero from the same district, he treats her with politeness. (He understands she's going to the cine.)

"Senora, I hope you sell them."

Somebody going by pushing a cart of refuse jostles her. Leaving the market she crosses the street. Sometimes men from the barrio come here or to the railroad station nearby. Jobs as porters or in the market carting refuse or cleaning up a stall when the proprietor closes for the night. Or they just hang around. But tonight she has recognized no one.

They are going down the street. Through a bar window she sees her husband. She thinks it's him. He's talking to someone, another man. He's been away someplace. She hasn't seen him for a while. Maybe she has something to tell him. But through the window the place, with the crowd of men at the bar, the noisy music, seems hostile. She doesn't want to risk it. Perhaps he's drunk. Or perhaps he would be angry, shamed if he saw her in there with the children. She hasn't told him what she is doing because it would hurt him.

She goes down the street, feeling alienated from him, lonely. Now she is on her way to the movie past the lighted stores. As she crosses a street she tells the little girl:

"Hold onto my skirt. My hands are tied up, I'm holding the box of mangoes."

At the same time—that is, in real time not movie time—the tourists are on their way to the cinema. We have left the hotel and are on our way down the main street, the main boulevard of the city among the passing crowd. This is a wide avenue lined with lighted shops, restaurants, trees. On the sidewalk there are peddlers, blind beggars, soldiers on leave. A man half-hidden in a circle of onlookers is selling a wind-up toy. There are the tourists wearing their masks. Street singers. Jugglers. We are surrounded by the gay images of carnival. To this rendezvous we are moving through a series of languages (the language of underemployment, the language of historical imperialism) down Alameda Street to the movie theater.

Finally we arrive.

There is a long line. People have gone in for the first showing.

It is necessary to wait. Slowly, aimlessly people fill in behind us. We are standing at the head of the line.

Meanwhile Maria has taken her stand on the sidewalk. She is also waiting, with the outspread box, with the playing children. We are looking down at her. There is nothing to do but see her— at the bottom of the pool.

This is the pool, the glade of Narcissus. At this moment the reflecting surface, the mirror, is broken.

But can it ever be broken?

■ The Barn Raising

We were on our way to register the plan for utopia at the town offices. You'll ask, what will happen then? We have every confidence the plan will go through, that ultimately it will be accepted. First of all there is nothing in the plan that is in any way destructive or damaging to the town, on the contrary. And secondly the way the town offices have been set up, the way the town structure has developed in recent years (the number of committees and agencies set up to consider such plans—called "the review process"—the number of questions that have to be raised) makes it more certain everyone understands it, and therefore the plan will have a greater chance of acceptance. (Of course it could be rejected.) Ultimately, the plan rests on consent. Or you could say, on rejection. There is an equal possibility of that. However, the way the town offices, agencies and committees, etc., now function ensures that the plan will be carefully screened. Without taking this into account it would be foolish to submit the plan in the first place. Especially a utopian plan.

There is another sense in which this increase in the number of committees makes it less likely to be accepted. That is, anyone who has possible interests against it will know about it. As opposing interests will be brought to bear through the prescribed channels, in the clear light of day, all the arguments can be brought out publicly by those opposing it. But this actually turns out to be an advantage, because it is rare that one is able to "sneak through" some plan. It will be made public anyway. People will find out. And then one is in a worse position.

We were driving, the five of us, in Mike's car, from the edge of town—which is natural countryside—to the town center. We were going to submit a plan at the town hall.

"We better hurry. We don't want to be late," Janet said. "The town offices close at four. Does Gladys leave the office promptly at four?" (Gladys is the town clerk.)

"Sometimes she goes home earlier," Howard said, sticking his head out the car window and smelling the sweet air.

It had been raining all spring. Today it was sunny. The trees were in leaf. And the stream, swollen with snowmelt, rushed and roared beside the road between its banks lined with pussy willows.

We were making the trip in Mike's car, a red, shiny 1956 Ford Falcon with chrome on the radiator and aerodynamic fins. The car went with a certain time period of music: bebop. He had done a ring job on it a couple of weeks before. It was running well. The radiator leaked slightly. He had tried to patch it with some kind of gunk, but it hadn't worked.

"That's why I'm going slow. I'd like to go faster but I don't want the engine to overheat." He had brought along a can, Mike told us. If the car heated up he'd just stop by the stream and fill the can up with water and pour it in the radiator.

We were passing through the countryside of the town. Some dairy farms—and places that had once been farms. We passed a Burger King, a condominium development, a Cumberland Farms convenience store.

We had stopped at Spud Baxter's garage. The gas nozzle was guzzling in the tank. He was wiping off his hands with a greasy rag, looking up at the old-fashioned roman numerals on the pump gauge as they wheeled around.

"How are things, Spud?"

"Fair to middling. What's that you got in the back seat?"

We explained that we had this plan for the town, the plan for utopia, and that we were on our way to the town offices to register it.

"God, in the old days we just *did* it—if something had to be done." He had been lying under a truck body. His shirt, pants, his cap and hands all had the same coating of grease. "I should think nowadays—hazarding a guess—it'd be pretty hard to get a plan for utopia *through.*"

We ran down for him the number of steps, boards, committees, and commissions necessary to expedite it, see it through. Ending with the statement: "Consent has been *mandated.*"

"I can see how you'd get the plan registered with Gladys—if you get there. I can see you maybe getting it through one or two of the selectmen . . . Drew maybe. Or Burt. But I don't know about this *general consent* . . . " Spud pushed back his cap, showing the borderline to the sphere of his head, the color of white marble.

He went on, "In the old days I used to know everybody. But now I don't know anybody. Hardly."

"It's a minimum plan. To prevent the town from going downhill any more than it is," Janet explained. "We know it'll take time, with all these mandated steps. That's why we're rushing over today. Just to get started.

"Don't know if you're going to get there. I hear the bridge is out. The stream's overflowed."

"How do you like the Falcon?" Spud asked Mike.

"Running." He explained how he'd done a ring job on it last week. They had a talk about that. "Radiator leaks some. But basically it's sound."

"It sure sounds good. At least the cylinders," Spud told Mike.

"These old engines were built to last. America made cars in those days. You gotta believe it."

We were on the road again, riding along. The swollen stream ran beside the road, or the road followed the stream. We had the window of the car open (because it was a rare sunny day after the rain). The wind was blowing through everyone's hair.

We had been working nights. Though we were tired after making the plan, we had washed up and made ourselves presentable. Janet had even taken off her dungarees and put on a skirt.

"I don't know if I look good enough to go to the town hall. That Gladys is a fancy dresser. Well, she dresses sensibly."

"Maybe I should have shaved," Will said. Both he and Howard wore beards.

"The town's going downhill," Mike said. "It's slipping fast."

"Slipping," Will agreed.

"There's a tendency to erosion," Howard said. "To deterioration, to deflection from the right direction. There's a good deal of backsliding on the town's part from the once excellent thing it was."

"Things are so bad already—the circumstantial reality—that we may not be able to do anything. We may get there too late."

"We've got to hurry."

"What a plan for utopia represents," Janet told them, "is the frame of mind of utopians."

We were riding along, riding along.

We passed a couple more abandoned dairy farms. Some more Cumberland Farms convenience stores. Another condominium subdivision. A cluster of dentists' offices.

We were coming to the top of a hill, and were surprised to see a crowd of people milling around on an open field. We figured it might be a farmer's market or maybe a circus they were setting up.

"Something's going on it looks like."

A bunch of cars were parked by a stone wall. There were some old buggies and several 1956 Ford Falcons.

We parked by the road, then walked uphill to join the crowd. We recognized most of them. These were all people we played volleyball with on Sundays. And we went contra dancing with them.

The barn's posts were already up. Lying half-hidden on the grass were the sides of the barn, each one a huge wooden rectangle about twenty feet by sixty.

"What's happening? What's happening?"

"A barn raising."

"Well, I'll be hornswoggled."

"Do you think we ought to stay?"

"We should go. We're rushing to make it to the town offices."

"Maybe we should see what's going on. It looks like things are moving pretty fast."

"Pleasant folks."

There was Jonathan and Susan and Liela. Susan was on the ground breastfeeding the baby. People were milling around.

Men and women, these people were pretty strong carpenters. Fairly strong poultry raisers, and generally pretty strong on all aspects of broccoli, carrots, and kale raising. And several of them had a band. But they had never helped us out much with the town plan. Or worried as much as we did about saving the town from its downward slide. The idea of making a utopian plan would have been beyond them.

"*Dolce fa' niente.* They live for pleasure," Howard said. "You can see that from the way they're standing around, digging the scene."

"These are our own people."

"These are our own people. Or are they?"

Now we were sitting on the grass drinking homemade brew with Susan and Liela and Jonathan. Standing beside us getting ready to help, already helping, or simply digging the scene, were Porky and Elizabeth and their baby. And Dorothea and Haselton and Blye. And beside us was Ginger, lying on a blanket with Ruy Blas. He had an earring dangling from his ear.

"Raising Harry's barn," Haselton said, sipping his brew.

"Looks like it," Mike said.

"How's your plan?" Ginger asked. "I know you've been working on it for months and months."

"Well, now we're rushing in with it. Before it's too late."

"What kind of a plan is it?" Haselton asked.

"It's minimalist," Howard told him. "Just planning for a little selected retrogression and rock-back-in-time, with a high-tech fix."

"You come to the right place," Haselton said.

It seemed to us there were about a hundred people up there on the hill but it could have been forty. The top had been cleared off. There was a monstrous bulldozer or earthmover or roadgrader, belching diesel smoke, that somebody had borrowed from the town garage.

"How's your car running, Mike?"

"The Falcon? How's yours?"

"What does Harry want the barn for?" Janet asked.

"Going to raise registered Belgian work horses," Ruy Blas said. "He wants every dairy farmer in Vermont to trade in his tractor for a horse. Save money in fertilizer."

"Well, Harry looks happy. Happy as Larry."

We went and stood by Harry and put our arm around him. He was a blond head taller than any of us. The framing was post and beam; he had done all the prefabrication work himself with a little help from Ruy Blas. Proprietor of the barn (or more properly, of a structure which when filled with hay and manure would become a barn). Harry had seen the structure rise many times in his head. He had not, mentally, foreseen this gathering of neighbors to put up the barn, as he had never told anybody. People from the smaller farms, the backroads, and trailer camps, people who knew how to raise barns and who remembered it had just come. Now all Harry had to do was stand there, smiling, in his suspenders.

At the moment, the bulldozer was perched, like a marooned boat on a pile of dirt, the operator, Ellis, sitting on it. On the flat place Coleman and the band members were setting up their amplifying equipment.

We were looking, shielding our eyes, into the sky. "Who's that? What's going on up there?" we asked Harry.

"That's Kelton. He's brought some rigging."

On the top of a very tall rickety ladder and stretched between the ladder and the post, was an old man in coveralls, thin and tall as a scarecrow, or like some long-legged heron.

"You know Kelton?"

We thought we had seen a photo of him ten years before in the newspaper, fixing the church roof.

"Famous steeplejack."

Another old man in striped coveralls and railroad cap was cutting a groove into an angle beam—or cutting a slot in the post so the angle beam would fit into it. He was also thin and frail. He had transparent skin and a soft cloud of white hair escaping from him. He was on his knees, squinting with pale blue eyes and knocking a chisel with a mallet. He seemed to be gauging the cut along the line of his nose and his lantern jaw.

"That's Lyman Goodall, the famous carpenter. Lyman or Layman . . . Goodall or Goodrich . . . "

We had a picnic once in the town cemetery and there had been a stone of that name. Probably the same family.

"You got quite a sprinkling of old timers here," I said.

Harry pointed to another, at the bottom of the posthole. All we could see was a huge pair of shoulders and a bald skull. Bent double, he was moving rock.

"That old man," Harry said, "can practically claw a rock out of the ground with his bare hands. See the hands?"

"Incredible."

"That's the legendary farmhand and handyman Mike Wheelock."

Halfway down the slope and uphill from the cars a line of tables had been set up. Here there was a line of women servers, all round as cats, in flowering print dresses, with elbows disappearing in the flesh and with benign doughy faces, getting ready to serve beans and apple pies.

People were taking their places along the timbered frame.

"Getting ready to push," Harry said.

We were all figuring—since we were here and at any rate weren't on the road and making some kind of progress toward utopia—we might as well help get the barn up.

At a signal from Wheelock, the musicians blasted loose. As they did so, we pushed. The four walls came up—naturally one wall at a time—everybody puffing and straining and shouting to each other to hold on. Except some of the smaller children who were playing ring-around-the-rosey in the grass. And some little boys blowing horns on the Falcons.

We were riding along, riding along. The fields were blooming, the stream was rushing between its banks of alders and pussy willows.

"That was a great scene," Howard said.

"Way out," Janet said.

"Sure makes you feel good," I said. "It charges the batteries."

"Did you notice all the farmers and elderly citizens, old types come out of the woodwork to help Harry? I thought they were all dead."

"Wonderful scene. Blew your mind."

"State of the Art of the Possible. Utopian in its own way . . . in kind of a minimalist way."

"Those people have no theoretical basis. All they know is practice," Howard said.

We passed another Cumberland Farms convenience store. Another Kentucky Fried Chicken. Another gas station.

"God, the water really is high."

"Maybe we should be going faster, maybe we shouldn't have stopped to help Harry."

"I'm sure going to be relieved," Will said, "what with the river overflowing and the engine heating up on the hills, when we make it to the top of the last hill. And see the town."

We were riding along with all the windows down. Miles Davis was playing on the car stereo.

Howard was puffing. "Ruy Blas gave me a hit of grass. You guys want some?"

Suddenly the car stopped. The door was open. Mike was out of it and rushing across the field.

"What's happening? What's with Mike?"

"I forgot to tell you," Janet said, "he's heavy into Catholicism. Sees visions."

"Not here."

"The other night we were at the movies. Song of Bernadette. It really blew his mind."

Mike was sprinting across the field. The high grass slowed him down some but he was still rushing forward, his arms raised. We were all watching from the car.

"Reason is the handmaid of Faith," Howard said. "Mystical."

"Age of Aquarius."

"He's going to take off."

Then it looked like he'd stumbled. He'd plunged forward. He was on his knees.

He came back in about five minutes.

"Mike, are you all right? We thought you were going to fall and break a leg."

"Incredible experience," Mike said. "I heard organ music."

"What was it?"

"Well, I was in the corn stubble. And she was before me."

"Who was?"

"Our Lady of Guadalupe. In a blue gown. She was smiling at

me. There were these rays radiating from behind her head."

"Well, now the car engine is steaming. Maybe we should get some water while we're here."

We had stopped at a bridge before the last hill. Mike and Will had gone down to the stream to fill the can and were pouring water in the radiator. There was an old man on the bridge leaning on the railing.

He was gazing down at the rush of water, which came almost up to the floorboards of the bridge, swirling and foaming. It looked like Kelton, but we weren't sure it was Kelton.

"River's full."

"So we've noticed."

"Up the banks."

"Over the banks."

"God, there's a lot of it, ain't there? Considerable snowmelt this year." He spit a long plume of tobacco.

We agreed there had been a lot of snowmelt.

"Road's not that certain up ahead. Where you boys from?" He asked us generally, tipping his hat to Janet. "I guess you're going toward the . . . the way you're headed."

We told him we were driving to the town hall.

"God, I dunno if you'll make it." The old-timer shook his head. "With all this *water*. I'm surprised you got this far."

We were going up the long, last, slow hill. From the top of it we would be able to see the town. Our town was a hillside town. It was a riverside town. Tumbling down from the crest of the hill, the town pushed right out to the bank. It was a wide turbid river. Many a time we'd sat there on the wharf at night and watched the steamboats slip by.

"God, I hope it's still there."

"Why wouldn't it be there?"

"I have this terrible feeling," Will said, "a kind of anxiety that comes from the pit of the stomach . . . a dread."

It may have been because on this last hill the radiator was about to boil over again. The gauge was at the top, there was the sound of bubbling. When Mike had stopped at the bridge the last time and unscrewed the cap to fill it, there had been a plume of steam, like a genie let out of a bottle. Now there was more steam.

Or it may have been we were anxious because we were late. We had wasted too much time stopping at Harry's barn. The town office could be closed and Gladys gone home.

Or it could be just the ups and downs of the ride, through the countryside of the town with its paranoid scenery: one-half dairy farms and pussy willows, one-half dentists' offices.

In any case, each of us felt this sense of impending doom hanging over the town. Though it was different in each case because we were probably seeing, thinking about, and imagining different towns. For Janet the town was at the bottom of the hill by the railroad flats, entangled in a network of rails, freight switchyards, or truck depots. A tank car had overturned and blown up. The town was in the process of being evacuated. A giant chemical disaster.

For Will it was in the way of some airport runway. It was at the edge of a big city—or had been at the edge and was being swallowed up and covered over with cement. For Mike or Howard maybe it had disappeared in a nuclear attack.

My own feeling was that it was too late. Not dramatically too late, or violently too late. It was just that we had taken too much time, gone too slow. Probably the reason was, we were too cautious, there was not much to look forward to—with all these committees.

My own nightmare, my own personal scenario for disaster was that the town had simply gotten bigger and bigger. The town was simply growing, developing in all directions, it was becoming musclebound and strangling itself, swelling and imploding due to its sheer size. At the same time, it was getting heavier and heavier, developing this enormous weight. So, as Spud had said, there was this danger of slippage.

Add to this the fact that it had been raining. The town was on this sidehill above the river, on this terminal moraine. There could have been a mudslide.

We had reached the crest. The Falcon was throwing off steam; a great billow of steam drifted into the sky. The sun caught it and shone on it. The sun which must have just been setting in the west behind Harry's barn illuminated it. Over the engine and over us hung this white billow of steam drifting away and dissolving. It was lovely.

We looked down. The town was gone.

■ The Changing Beast

The food co-op had been meeting to discuss the future of the co-op. We had decided to open a store. This would be on the main street of the town of McIndoe Falls and would provide the town with organic food.

"Because it's on the main street," someone said, "everyone will come in. America craves healthy food."

This decision was made by consensus. Everyone agreed. There had been objections, disputes. At one point Betsy Morrison had blocked consensus, in tears, holding us up for several hours.

"Why should we change? We haven't been a store before. We've just been a group of people who work hard and like each other. We haven't been customers."

We put our arms around her, comforted her, told her how much we respected and loved her. Her holding out was part of it, the process. "But this is part of it . . . your feelings . . . that you are holding out on us, in tears."

Bernie in particular, his arm over Betsy's shoulder, gave her an extra squeeze.

"Anyway," Jake said, "it has to be a decision we can all live with, we can all be comfortable with."

This was how we decided to open a store.

We were spending the evening at Swallows' Nest. Every month our co-op would meet at a different household. Someone would read out the items, and each household would order its supply of organic food. A couple of times a year we would volunteer to put in an afternoon or evening at the central co-op warehouse in McIndoe, on "break-down," that is, dividing up the food as it came in the truck from the wholesalers in Boston, weighing it out and measuring it and putting it into bags or boxes marked for the different groups or households.

But interest had been declining. People were dropping out for one reason or another, and we had fewer people to do the work.

It was a March night at Swallows' Nest, the farmhouse where Joanne and Chuck lived. Semolina had read out the list of food items, fruits and grains. People would decide what they wanted for the next month and in what quantities. That would be our bulk order. Semolina, who was tall anyway, sat on a tall stool with her straight hair and marked everything down.

We were in a comfortable circle around her and the stove, most of us in stocking feet. Chuck was in the stuffed armchair, his arm around Joanne, who was breast-feeding the baby. Teacups were in the sink and left-over carrot cake and ginger cookies were in the pan. Seedlings were being started in pots. The floor was cluttered with other small children and dogs.

Betsy said, "It seems so *natural* this way. This is the best way . . . the way we are. Just friends. We've been a network . . . a food cooperative I guess you'd call it. But local and friendly."

Betsy had felt strongly enough about this proposition to block consensus, in tears. We all liked Betsy. She was our favorite person—if there was a favorite person. I think consensus could have been easily blocked; she might have swung it the other way—if it had not been for Chuck. Chuck was extremely determined about everything he thought must be done. And he could persuade us.

Anyway we were sitting around the stove and Betsy was talking about just ordering food with each other and being friends.

Chuck said, "Sure, that stage of our lives was okay. It was beautiful. But it was one stage. And now we're going on to another stage."

Judy said, "We're going from the cooperative stage to the outreach stage. Providing service."

"We've all agreed on the change," Chuck told her. "And you, Betsy, agreed—when you saw the logic of it."

"Still," Betsy said, "there's a danger."

That was the first night we were visited by the beast. We had been sitting in the living room around Semolina and the stove, and the beast had been outside in the snow, looking in. Lonely and cold, coming out from the wilderness, it must have been attracted by the conviviality of the group. Reared up on its hind legs, its muzzle pressed against the glass. Our light must have shone out through the frosty panes into its eyes. The smells of the room where the co-op was meeting and the sound and murmur of our words must have drifted through the window into its nostrils and ears.

When we came out later we saw its tracks.

We had taken over the abandoned mill. It was beside the falls, at the edge of town where the highway ran into McIndoe. It had been a sawmill in the wilds, then a window and sash manufactory, during the Depression a shirtwaist factory. It was a sizable red brick building.

Below, the river was roaring by. We had finished renovating the interior; we were about ready to open the store.

"That's the Allagogash River roaring by beating against the foundation," Judy said, stretching out her arms. "Feel the energy." She felt the energy flowing through her circulatory system like prickly heat. It started at the floorboards of the old mill at the soles of her feet, coursed up through her haunches and buttocks into her chest, and suffused her face, like steam coming off a plate of soup, coloring her face like a rose. Judy retied the bandanna around her red hair.

The sight was dazzling. I had always been crazy about Judy.

There was a general blooming of energy in the room among the cooperators. Recently we had suffered a loss of energy, but this was a resurgence. It came from all of us, from everyone working at the common task with their bodies, from the beauty and solidity of the old building, and from the shine and brilliance of the floor we had just been polishing.

We looked at it, admiring our work.

"This place is too big for us, for the group," Joel remarked. "We're small now. The movement is small . . . the organic movement. But someday we'll be feeding all of New England, when the rest of the country collapses. The system's bound to collapse sooner or later. Trucking lettuces and brussel sprouts from the Salinas Valley in a refrigerator truck burning diesel oil . . . It's crazy. We'll start small, then we'll get bigger. But we'll always stay an appropriate size. Our vegetables will always be fresh." It was Bernie who was saying this.

"The whole economy will collapse—we'll be sitting on it," Jake said, looking up at the ceiling. "But we'll keep tight. We'll stay together and keep loving each other."

We were all in a circle.

"Let's all hold hands," Betsy said. "I have a feeling I'd like us all to hold hands."

The name of our cooperative store was to be The Total Planet.

POETRY OF THE STORE / THE STORE VANDALIZED

The store was opened for business. Crowds flowed through. The long space of the mill floor had been divided into aisles to direct the flow of customers through the store, to guide them and to focus their eyes. Along a top shelf there was a line of the brightest blue buckets with white tops, these containing pulses in bulk: split peas, chick-peas, yellow-eyed peas, and black turtle beans. On the shelf below a row of white buckets with green tops containing pastas and macaroni of many kinds. On the opposite shelf an enticing display of clear bags containing seedless raisins and multiple assorted nuts: cashews, almonds, walnuts, butternuts, and filberts, and bags showing off granolas and several kinds of trail mix. On the right as you entered there were unadorned boxes of homegrown potatoes stained with earth, knobby carrots, ginseng roots, and assorted natural apples with the original spots of scale. Then the customer passed by the glass doors of the refrigerator behind which were fresh leafy vegetables beaded with dew, organic fruit juices, cheeses of all kinds and yogurts: Rosedale, Blithedale, Sunnydale, Brown Cow, Stoney Hill Farm, and Butterworks Acidophilus. At one side was an alcove for rest, where the children could play with blocks and puzzles, and a sofa where you could read the latest news and look up at a poster of coffee pickers in Nicaragua.

Finally there was an oaken desk—which in a regular store

would be the checkout counter—where the staff person stood exchanging the news of the day as she tallied up items and prices. There was a calendar of events and a volunteers' sign-up sheet. The wall behind us was a dazzling display, floor to ceiling, of multicolored Celestial Seasoning herb tea boxes.

All this was wrecked.

Judy, who was the staff person, came in early one morning. She telephoned everyone announcing the disaster. "It's total destruction of the Total Planet," everyone was told. "You can come over and look at it."

The rest of us came and looked at it. It was a wreck. Totaled, as Judy had said. Pulses and pastas on the floor, buckets of oats, barley, and millet tipped over, thrown around and trampled on. Bags of organic candies and assorted nuts split open, safflower and sesame oil spilled, granola and barrels of rice flour scattered over the floor. In the alcove the poster was torn down and the sofa chewed.

"It's total destruction! Or almost."

Someone said, "Hostile teenagers? I saw some around, high on speed. Maybe we should call the police."

"No, I think it was some kind of animal. Not a skunk because this destruction doesn't have that skunky flavor, it's kind of rank. Could it be a raccoon?"

"A cow? The tracks."

"Christ, a cow couldn't have climbed up into the mill."

"It's a big one all right," Jake said, looking at the tracks. "Check out those paw marks . . . or is it hoof marks? This is a peculiar animal."

All over the floor were marks that looked like the paws of a bear. And in the granola and mashed splotches of tofu, what looked like the hoof marks of a goat.

"This is the same animal that's been out to get us from the beginning."

"A ruminant," Chuck said. "A herbivore or a carnivore?"

"This one just barged in. It has a destructive animus."

"A large animal. That's all you can tell about it . . . not its kind or its shape."

"If it *is* an animal. Whatever it is, it's hostile and bestial."

Bernie and I had decided that Chuck was the beast. There had been signs of this before, while we had been working fixing up the site, that some presence had been prowling around at night. There would be the marks of the beast, signs and footprints—or rather hoof prints. In general, animal droppings and litterings. During the construction Chuck was always encouraging us, bullying us and urging us to work harder. We remembered too that when Betsy had blocked consensus on the store—and might have carried the day because she felt so deeply—it was Chuck who had persuaded us.

Bernie said, "He has an aggressive quality, a relentless logic to him. In these meetings you're not supposed to *persuade*."

We were having a meeting. Now that the store had been vandalized, Chuck wanted to make the operation bigger, expand. "Bigness is what we need, largeness. It's the amplitude and largeness of the operation that permits economies of scale. We need a dock to unload the larger trucks from the wholesaler's. We used to have small trucks . . . small trucks, jeeps, and pick-ups. Farmers bringing in food, the local produce. Corn in season, rushing in with the first strawberries. Bartering . . . exchanging. Now we've gotten beyond that."

Bernie and I were sitting with Betsy and Judy. I told them, "I think Chuck is the beast. And Bernie thinks so too."

"Is there a beast?"

"Of course, everybody knows that. He first appeared at the farmhouse looking in the window when we were deciding about the store. It's true, nobody's seen him, he's been hiding. At night he has a beast's shape. But during the day he could be Chuck. He could change his shape."

"I don't see why you think it's a *he*," Judy said. "That it's a male."

It was twilight in the old mill. I had noticed this peculiar smell coming from Chuck. It may not have been a goat smell—as Bernie had suggested. But it wasn't a human smell either. The back of his hands and wrists were very hairy. He had been waving mosquitoes away while he was talking, and they were all coming over and landing on us.

"What's necessary," Chuck was telling us, "in order to effect economies of scale, cost-effectiveness, competitive wholesaling, is a rationalized transportation network and all that. We've gone through that, with the expanded parking lot. Then we went into the next phase—plant and equipment, stockpiling, inventory. Now we go into bookkeeping, with the restoration of the store. There's double-entry bookkeeping, cross-totaling, computerized bookkeeping."

A bat flew over our heads.

"I got to pee," Chuck said.

I looked over at Bernie. He gave me the high sign.

We followed Chuck out the door, out toward the stream bank and over by a clump of blackberries. This seemed to us an excellent place to turn into a beast. Bernie and I held back at a safe distance, but close enough to be able to see, to take in and to monitor what was happening.

But nothing happened. That night nothing happened by way of transformations. All Chuck did was pee over the bank. And then we went back with him. We were still thinking it could be Chuck. It had just been at the wrong time. The beast didn't like to change his shape, to make his transformations when anybody was watching.

We were on a hill waiting for the beast. Betsy had borrowed Semolina's shotgun. Semolina grew marijuana on her hilltop farm, hidden among the poplar saplings, and kept the gun in the event of a raid.

Members of the co-op had been out several nights stalking the beast, tracking him and waiting for him to appear so we could shoot him. Betsy had the shotgun on the ground beside her, at the moment unloaded. There were the three of us, me, Bernie, and Betsy, lying on a picnic blanket in a clump of low-bush blueberries. We were in the shadow of an oak, moonlight filtering down through the leaves.

"Do you think the beast will show himself on a night like this?"

"What do you mean?" I asked Bernie.

"Maybe it's too bright. The beast only shows himself in obscurity."

Judy, who was my own love, and Betsy had been going up to Semolina's to help her with her woodlot. She logged with horses.

Betsy had announced to us, at the end of the last co-op meeting, that she was going to live with Semolina.

Betsy was telling us how she had first fallen in love with Semolina. "I came up to bring something, I forget what. Anyway she had just come back from logging and had turned out the horses. We were standing by the pasture gate. There was a black mare with two foals. They were running across the field, through the high grass. Semolina said: 'There's no more beautiful sight than a mare galloping over a field. A black mare with shiny flanks, slick from the logging work. She'll be running over the field at full speed for no other reason than to stretch her neck out into the wind. She'll turn like a freight train shaking the ground, thundering like a train coming around the bend—only in tighter and tighter circles . . .' That's when I decided I was in love with Semolina and I wanted to always be with her."

She went on telling me and Bernie about the relationship, or series of relationships. Recently the waitress from the McIndoe cafe had come up to join them.

Bernie kept sheep. He'd tried logging.

"So how is it up there? All that women's space?" Bernie asked miserably.

"You mean about the *relationships*? There are certain relationships that a woman can only have—I mean, deeply and completely—with another woman. All my life I've been on the *brink* of discovering that but it never happened."

"Like what?" Bernie asked her.

"You mean an example? Well, it's hard . . . I mean it's really difficult to be friends with a man, probably it's impossible. But there's nothing more sacred . . . I mean in a relationship between two people, than friendship. I mean, it's a state of being *yourself* . . . that can just be taken for granted."

"Uh-huh," Bernie grunted.

The three of us were lying there on the blanket, Bernie squeezed in between me and Betsy.

I felt myself I was going to roll off, down the hill. Bernie felt (while Betsy was telling us all this) the pressure of Betsy's arm against him, partly resting over his shoulder. He could feel her hair in his face, her chin resting on the blanket, the top of her head and the sweet smell of it, under his nose. He could feel his own arm partly pushing the length of Betsy's arm, chest, and waist, which was covered by a wool sweater, pressing against them, the warmth of them making him slightly tingle. And downwards from this point the pressure of his hip against Betsy's hip, his knee against her knee and his lower calf against her lower calf covered with worn blue jeans. It was this pressure, the close proximity of Betsy lying in a bed of blueberries, that tried him. The whole of him—the bodily Bernie as opposed to the listening and sympathizing Bernie—was tingling, prickling, and burning as if lit by an illicit fire, which aroused him and levitated him at certain points. He would have liked to roll over on top of her and crush her mouth like strawberries.

It was then that we saw the beast.

"Look! Jesus!" Betsy exclaimed.

The beast was not fifty feet away from us and was looking down in the direction of the town of McIndoe. Unaware of us, he was probably musing about the mill. We were at the back of him, but we could see the front part, covered with brown fur. It had a long snout and teeth stained with blueberries. The ears stuck up sharp. It had the muzzle and paws of a bear. At the back there was a rump which stuck up, its haunches covered with long shaggy grey and black hair—matted and streaked, as disreputable as the beard of an old wino who'd been in the street all night. Below the haunch, from the knee down to the hooves, was black, like he was wearing boots. Underneath the rump, between the legs, a huge sack hung down covered with hairs and almost dragging on the ground.

Bernie said in awe, "The front part's bear. And the back part's ram. A Hampshire ram."

A HOT PURSUIT

Jake and Joel had been drinking beer in the McIndoe Cafe. Joel was the one who had found the mill, when the co-op had been planning its outreach. A perfect place, right in the town of McIndoe.

On the way home they saw the beast. He was in the A & P parking lot.

"There he is!" Joel shouted, grabbing Jake's arm. "Let's follow him." This is how they told the story later to the co-op.

The animal had gone around the corner of the supermarket toward the back. For a while they thought they had lost him. They came on him again, quite close, by a row of garbage cans. He was moving forward smelling things, sniffing them, exploring them with great curiosity.

"He's into the cans," Jake said. "The beast is so preoccupied with garbage he doesn't see us."

They were able to watch the beast (and describe it to the other members of the cooperative later). With his nose he would pry up the lid or simply push the can over, stick his head in or pull out the contents with his paws, his eyes shifting and moving from item to item greedily, tearing it apart and fooling with it: rotten cabbages, lettuce leaves, meat bones, coffee grounds. He was continually moving, the back part propelled him on. While the head browsed and fed, the powerful hindquarters of the beast moved him forward over the yard of the supermarket, over the asphalt, his balls dragging on the ground.

"This animal is really gross," Jake told the other members of the co-op gathered around them. "Insatiable appetite for the supermarket waste."

"At the same time," Joel told them, "propelled forward by this tremendous dynamism. The beast is a monument to greed. Disreputable. The back side—the *motor* of the beast—is almost a sexual drive. Or scatological: pissing and defecating over everything and ready to fuck everything."

"He walks alone. He hunts alone. No group feeling here. The teeth the cutting edge. While the customers are out front he's gorging himself out back."

"Then what happened?" the rest of the group wanted to know.

"Well, we didn't have Semolina's gun. Not even a stick. We thought we had him penned in, cornered. We'd been tracking him, gradually approaching him and catching up with him. At this point he was right behind the back door of the A & P. There's a fenced area where they throw all the boxes out, mountains of boxes. There was a Dempster Dumpster, full of garbage. We were moving cautiously toward him; we were going to capture him and wrestle with him. We were going to bind him . . . "

"What happened?"

"As we went for him we lost him behind the dumpster," Jake said. "We went around there. Thought at first he'd crawled into the dumpster. But he wasn't in there. I crawled up to look. Disappeared clean as air. When I came down there was only the manager of the A & P standing there. Guess he'd just come out the door."

The manager of the A & P, a Mr. Belfast, was a man of about 5 feet 8 inches high, with all his hair. If he was remarkable for nothing else, the curliness, bushiness, and redness of Mr. Belfast's hair was remarkable. This showed the vigor of the man, untouched by the cares of the supermarket, which might have turned the hair of a younger man prematurely grey. The head, even when he went outside during the winter months, did not need to wear a hat, though it sometimes sported earmuffs. Inside the store the body of the man could be seen patrolling the floor in shirt-sleeves and a white apron. These shirts, which sported elastic armbands, were always smooth and white, the particular quality of whiteness set off by the redness and corrugated quality of Mr. Belfast's neck.

We have now adequately described the person of the store manager, except to say that he wore metal-framed octagonal glasses with which he peered at food items. In the pocket of his smock he carried a labeling and pricing gun.

To the customers of the store he presented a studious and preoccupied air, as he bent down over the shelves stamping the prices with the gun or marking down the items to reorder on his clipboard. Or he would raise his head and straighten his back in a smiling gesture as some customer came down the aisle approaching him, remark on the weather or exchange the town's news and gossip.

DEVELOPMENT OF THE PLOT

The manager, a father of five and a church elder in the McIndoe Falls church, has fallen in love with Judy, and occasionally visits her at the Total Planet, when he can find time. He enters briskly, setting in motion the string of bronze bells and setting the Nicaraguan coffee-pickers poster to flutter, and makes his way straight to where Judy is weighing out orders at the desk—his face flushed.

On this particular day he is carrying a pot of geraniums transported from the supermarket across the street, their petals red, lavender, and pink.

To the other members of the co-op watching him, the behavior of the older man—fired with desire—is somewhat ludicrous. Though we respect Judy's politeness and friendliness.

Secretly I ask myself: Do I envy him? Is she attracted to him as a father figure?

After a quarter hour's animated talk at the counter the manager leaves. On the way out, passing down the aisles, he bends down and adjusting his glasses, notes the various items of organic food and their prices. Sometimes he will pay us a compliment.

The A & P supermarket has begun to stock organic food items in its fresh produce section: leafy vegetables, tasty pesticide-free tomatoes and carrots. Even *tempeh* and *tofu*—we are told by our customers.

"I suspected this guy of treachery," Chuck exclaimed. "The minute he came in here, making eyes at Judy."

I say, "Masqueraded as a father figure."

"He's not interested in organics. Total Planet means nothing to him."

"The sonofabitch ripped us off!" Joanne said. "Now he's got everything we've got. And his prices are cheaper."

Jake said, "Anyway, Belfast is the beast. Or the beast has become Belfast. We almost caught him at it—when we were tracking him behind the supermarket. First we thought it was Chuck. Anyway we thought it was some one of us, who was a friend and cooperator during the day and at night changed his shape, or her shape, and was trying to fuck us over. There were all those hoof marks, and then vandalizing the store."

Semolina said, "Belfast is the real beast. He's *out there*. We have to deal with him."

Chuck had tried several times to shoot Belfast as he went by, with Semolina's gun. There was no effect. The man or beast who was Belfast simply kept walking on his own side of the street and went in to his job at the A & P.

"Semolina's gun isn't working," Chuck told Joanne.

The cooperative was having a stormy meeting about the phase of retrogression they were in now.

Bernie said, "We could try picketing the store."

We went through all the slogans, all the picketing signs we could write.

Patronize Your Locally Grown Store. Keep Your Dollars in McIndoe.

Enforce Ethical Pricing.

Develop Planet Consciousness. Shop at Total Planet.

Competition Is Not a License For Theft & Murder.

The A & P Is Flea-Ridden.

"Have these economic boycotts ever worked?" someone asked. "We would only be calling attention to them."

"The A & P? It's half the size of the town of McIndoe."

"It's Belfast we should be appealing to. Couldn't we confront Belfast, as a person?" Betsy suggested.

"I can't see what that would do," Chuck objected. "It's true, Belfast is a nice guy. He's head of the Four-H Club, he's an elder of the church and all that. And he has this attraction to Judy— which is all in his favor. Personally he's okay. But his position in the system is to screw us. Functionally speaking—as an employee—he's deadly."

"I still think he's a sweet person. He brought flowers . . . "

"He's a commodity fetish, he's been mystified by the system."

"There are a thousand middle managers like Belfast."

"No. It's the man we have to deal with."

"This is the beast within the man."

"He may like us," Joanne said, "but he has to be on the other side. Against us."

"His mind has been fucked over. Brainwashed."

"Belfast is a beast in thrall."

We decided to confront Belfast, to capture him and debrief him.

"No violence," Betsy warned us. She was mostly worried about what Semolina would do once she got in there.

"We don't want to break anything in the store."

THE RAID ON THE A & P

"I really hate to go in there," Joanne said.

The co-op stood in front of the doors of the A & P. It was shortly after closing time. We had watched the last customers trundle their shopping carts over the parking lot and drive home.

"I'll tell you," Jake said, "I haven't been in one of these places in years. A supermarket. Avoided them like the plague."

Chuck was eyeing the doors. He remarked, "They're dangerous. These doors open automatically, by vacuum. Vacuumatic. Stand too close to them and you get sucked in."

We peered through the plate glass into the supermarket. It was empty, flooded with light.

"When were you in one of these places last?" Jake asked Joanne.

"It was before the baby was born. These places are completely dehumanizing." Joanne was carrying the second baby in a back-strap. The older toddler held her hand. There were several other children.

Now we were standing inside.

"Will you smell it! Is it the floorwax . . . or Lysol? Or is it the air-conditioning system?"

"This place is huge. It's as big as a football field or hockey rink. You could rollerskate in here."

The space seemed to stretch out for miles.

"A non-smell," somebody said. "A non-taste and a non-smell. It's neutralized."

"This place is a low energy sink."

We were standing in the front by the checkout area. There were no employees on the floor. In the general emptiness several of the remaining checkout girls, in smocks, sat at the counters, before the cash register, their heads nodding under the computer screen.

"They're sleeping. . . . In the silence and emptiness. It's weird."

One of the families with small children had put one in a shopping cart and was pushing it.

Joel said, "We want to find Belfast, but we don't want to get lost ourselves. I think we should stay together whatever we do. What do you think, Semolina?"

"No, we should split up into searching parties. But even then . . . This place is so huge . . . "

It was at that moment that we saw Belfast.

In the far distance a functionary appeared, around a corner. We watched the figure grow larger. He was trundling a dolly or wheeled cart loaded with boxes. The man was stooped and wore a green smock. He advanced silently till he came to a larger open space, the intersection point with one of the aisles. Here there was a pile of boxes, beverage containers. He unloaded the cart, transferring the cartons to the top of the other pile, and stepped back to look at it as if he were arranging some sort of display.

"It's Belfast!" Semolina and Judy both shouted together. "Catch him!"

The manager, after looking up quickly, had begun to run down the aisle.

"Follow him!" The entire cooperative took off in the direction of the abandoned dolly. When we turned and started down the side aisle—which was Beverages and Soft Drinks—we saw the manager running at full speed down the end of it. He turned the corner and disappeared.

Jake, Joel, Semolina, and Betsy, and the mother with the infant in the shopping cart were ahead, but everyone was following. We expected to find him at the back of the supermarket where the Dairy and Cheese section ran along the wall, maybe stealing along the freezers. He had eluded us.

"Where is he?"

"Slippery sonofabitch."

"There he is!" Someone had sighted the manager at the far end of the next aisle over. He was barely in sight. Now we were running up the next aisle: Canned Vegetables and Instant Soups.

"Which way did he go, left or right?"

"He's fast!"

"Maybe we should split into two groups."

"Down the next aisle!!"

The group had barreled down the Gourmet Foods, Salad Dressing, and Ketchup aisle, the manager out in front. Then down the Cold Cereals, Paper Towels, Tooth Pastes and Shampoos, and Sanitary Napkin aisle. And then down Cake Mixes and Baking Needs, the manager sprinting ahead. We were back at the checkout counters again.

"There he is! In Dog Foods!"

We were all running down the center aisle. At the end of it we saw Belfast at the wall. He had come to a halt in front of a huge display marked Organic Foods.

"Now we got him! Close in on him!"

"No violence," Betsy shouted. She threw herself on Semolina. I had Joanne around the waist.

"Be careful, don't let him bite you. Remember, he's a beast."

The manager was throwing items of organic food, lettuces, cabbages, heads of broccoli, then a whole container of yogurt. This he was doing to cover his retreat. He was retreating backward from us, throwing produce, edging along the wall. Then he stepped out through a back door.

We went out also through the door. But there was nothing to be seen. No manager. Deserted. This was the warehouse area, cold, dark, and endless. There were endless lines of packing crates forming corridors—in these, forklifts. Running the length of the ceiling was an overhead loading track.

The group was sure the manager had given them the slip, when suddenly he was seen again going out the sliding door to the rear, which led out to the truck loading bay. The group rushed outside following on his heels and into the back of a truck. It was a trailer which had been unloading, its motor running. But when we rushed in there after him, there were only the bare walls. The manager was nowhere to be seen.

The doors were slammed shut from outside. The truck drove off.

A NIGHT RIDE

We had been riding along in total darkness across several states, the members of the co-op sleeping on the bottom of the truck. There were only the sounds of the highway.

Finally we could feel the truck slowing to a stop. "Truck stop," Semolina said.

We heard the bolts grating in the outer lock. The back door swung open. We stood looking down at the truck driver.

"Here he is. The new beast," Joel said.

Jake said, "I knew when we ran in here, after the manager, when we ran him to ground in the truck and there wasn't anything in there but a blank wall . . . I thought he was going to change his shape."

"There isn't any Belfast. He was just a metaphor for capitalism."

"Now we have this new shape."

We were looking down at the truck driver. And the truck driver was looking up at us.

"Well, we're still wrestling with him," Joanne said. "Only this time he's got us. We're somewhere out West . . . Ohio maybe . . . at a truck stop."

The driver invited the Total Planet in for coffee.

Next we were at a table inside the diner, surrounded by other truck drivers. The driver was treating us to scrambled eggs and coffee.

Judy: "I think the new beast is quite a nice person actually . . . treating us to breakfast somewhere in Indiana. Or wants to be—is trying to be—a nice person. Though I don't like his looks. And he pinched me under the table and tried to run his hand up my behind."

Betsy: "He did that to me too."

Joel: "Like a sailor when he hits port, when he's on land. You'll find that your American truck driver at a truck stop is at his worst. But on the road he's an impressive figure. He's larger than himself. He's larger and faster than real life."

THE NEW BEAST DESCRIBED

The truck driver: a man of the open road. Is he a proletarian? It is not known what an American proletarian looks like. This one is stockier, squatter than Belfast. But he has Belfast's corrugated neck and red skin. The subject has a barrel chest, large belly. Belly compressed against the driving wheel. On the road, feet growing out of the brake and clutch pedals. Hands easy on the wheel. Substantial molars but missing front teeth, from which toothpick protrudes. As the miles go by he listens to the CB radio blasting. His head an empty movie house of dreams. Cap stuck around with Brotherhood of Teamsters' Union buttons.

What is he dreaming of? He is dreaming of coming home to Texas, to Abilene. After six days and nights on the transcontinental road circumnavigating the semi-globe.

Now we are on the roadway. (The co-op is allowed in the cab one at a time to keep the driver company.) Bernie is talking to the truck driver:

"Own your own rig?"

"Couldn't keep up the payments."

"That's the way it goes. What were you before?"

"A cowpuncher."

"You don't say?"

"It's all the same ride, when you're driving for someone else. Now I drive for MegaContinental, a division of Proteus."

"What's Proteus? Seems to me I've heard of it."

"It's on the stock exchange. Some fucking energy conglomerate. Energy . . . transportation. . . . These companies are all the same."

"Yea," Bernie says. "They absorb other energy companies."

"They're all shit," the truck driver says.

There was the giant hum of the giant eighteen-wheeler truck. Heat of the engine rising through the floorboards. The radio blasting out country music as the highway rolled by. There was a plastic medal of Saint Christopher dangling over the mirror.

"Comfortable in here," Bernie says. It was like a cave. The cave of myth.

"What do you think about during all these hours on the road?"
"Pussy."

They were going through corn country, the heartland of America. A sea of corn lapping against the sides of the truck.

In the back of the truck there were the rest of us. We could breathe through the door cracks. It was not too uncomfortable. We were sitting on the padded mats they use to move the crates when they pack them during the night, the early morning hours, in all the market terminals which coexist with all the cities. It was cold and dark, but it wasn't that cold.

"This beast's head is full of sexual fantasies," Judy said. "I suppose you've noticed?" At the truck stops we were allowed out to pee, and the mothers could fill up their baby bottles with milk, be treated to cups of coffee, talk with him, and suffer the advances of the new beast.

"We're a long way from McIndoe."

"Hang on, group. We're wrestling with the beast."

We were lying on the crates (a load of mushrooms we had picked up in Emmaus, Pennsylvania, the first night. And boxes of organic tomatoes we had picked up the second night in Ohio.). Semolina, with her feeling of restlessness, was standing with a flashlight, reading out the list of shipments from the manifest posted on the wall.

"We've picked up mushrooms and tomatoes in Pennsylvania and Ohio. That's what it says here. The Boston Produce Market is on the top of the list. The second stop was McIndoe where they delivered all that stuff, where they ripped us off. I guess (Semolina peered close with the flashlight; the print was close and the truck bed was swaying) the next stop is Kansas, that's hybrid corn. Then we're headed down south, Texas, where we're taking on a load of organic rice and onions in Deef Smith County. Then for whole grains to Arrowhead Mills."

"That's Deef Smith County, Texas," Jake said. "The organics capital. They're worth millions. Looks like the A & P has absorbed the total organics market."

"It says here," Semolina said, peering and squinting, "at the top of the manifest . . . the A & P is owned by MegaContinental, a division of Protean Enterprises."

We picked up another passenger. We were crossing Nebraska. A figure was flagging the truck down. "See him?" Chuck asked the driver. "Someone in distress."

We were in the rolling wheat country. The burgeoning wheat country, the big sky wheat country. Waves of wheat were lapping against the hubcaps.

The truck driver stopped and told him to climb in the cab.

The man said he was an arbitrageur from New York.

"What's an arbitrageur?" the truck driver asked, not turning down the radio. It was going full blast and the heat from the plains penetrated the cab.

"We arrange mergers, consolidations. We buy and sell companies."

"I hear," Chuck told him (this was information from the manifest) that A & P has been bought out by MegaContinental, a division of Protean Enterprises.

"MegaContinental *was* owned by Exxon. And Arrowhead Mills *was* owned by Cargill. But they've both been consolidated into Protean. Now there's only one company left. I'm out of a job."

"Where you headed?"

"I'm trying to get to the West Coast, to L.A."

We were stretched out on a pile of grain sacks on the bed of the truck.

"If we'd stayed back in McIndoe at the store—I mean, if we'd stayed small," Jake said, "we wouldn't have had to wrestle with the beast."

"Everyone has to wrestle with the beast," Semolina said.

We had been having a meeting of the co-op as the truck lurched and had come to a consensus on this.

"Well, we're all here. Total Planet is here. The important thing is to hang on," Betsy said, "and keep loving each other. If we all keep loving each other and we keep hanging on, we'll outlast the beast."

I was hanging on to Judy. And Bernie was hanging on to Betsy. The level of energy was high. It was moral energy and spiritual energy. But most of all I could feel the physical energy, which was amplified by the vibrations of the truck and the loud country music coming from the cab. Bernie was in a state of bliss, lying between Betsy and Semolina. I was in a state of bliss. Judy was lying against me on the grain sacks, her arm around my waist to keep us from rattling. Joanne was on the other side of me. I had my arm around her. I had always been crazy about Joanne too. I was glad to get rid of Chuck, that he was up front in the cab.

"Total Planet is still riding," I said. "And we'll win."

In front in the cab the CB radio was blasting. There was the truck driver. Chuck was next to the driver. Next to him was Belfast. Next to him the banker. In the corner was the beast, Proteus. He was large, there was hardly room for him, especially his hooves. His paws were around the banker. He was enjoying himself, especially the noisy power of the truck, the speed. He had his head out the window, his muzzle into the cool air, the wind.

Then it was night. We were passing the lights of all the cities of America and the waving corn.

Now the truck driver was sleeping, in the bunk above us at the back of the cab. The beast was driving.

■■■ The Warehouse

1

Barbara and I were among the 20 million Americans who took part in the Hunger Chain. The chain from San Diego, California, through the Midwest to Bath, Maine. To be part of such an unprecedented aggregation of Americans, simply the immensity of it, is mind-boggling. One thinks these days in large numbers; the mind is continually occupied by them: as, the numbers of voters in the last election, the numbers of trucks on the highway, the miles traveled by astronauts. Or, more pertinently, the sheer number of inhabitants of the globe who have a substandard diet which was why the demonstration was organized in the first place. To be one among the many, all of whom had the same lofty idea—this, as I say, is mind-boggling.

We drove out of Fort Wayne, Indiana, to the valley, not a great distance. (For Barbara and me it was convenient.) We could see on the maps that this was where the line was to go. Roughly it was running west to east. Of course the overall line wasn't that straight (although it went straight across the desert and some of the plains states). Generally it followed the topography of the land, the slope and character of a given area: it was designed to blend into the regional landscape. Our valley is mostly rolling farmland with low hills and open fields, sandy soil (you've heard of the famous Sand County Almanac). The land mostly in corn and tomatoes. The Sandy River meanders down the center. And beside that the state highway.

There were parties leaving from the city by bus (of course there were parties who didn't leave at all, simply stayed home—

indifferent to, ignoring, in fact actually disliking the Great
Hunger Chain). Barbara and I drove out in her Honda. We had
picked out a spot, a location. There were no assigned places in
the line, though this could easily have been done. The day before
there had been a suggestion in the paper about where the line
might be weak, in need of reinforcements—because the sur-
roundings were uninteresting or because of the difficulty reach-
ing it. We headed for one of these. As we approached, we were
surprised to see activity along the route. Our section was already
sketched in. People had come early and tentatively taken up
positions along the line where the Hunger Chain was scheduled
to be. There were picnickers beside the road, groups of people
talking and joking, families and church groups or just couples
like ourselves. All of us had chosen the same spot. One of the
less attractive spots. But now the attraction was the people them-
selves, those of us who were there.

The mood was pretty upbeat. We were at the bottom and had
a clear view up the valley on either side. The whole valley was
taken up, successfully *marked* by the line. You couldn't see peo-
ple actually holding hands; the distance was too great. There had
been thin spots but these had evidently been reinforced. There
was particular interest in where it went through a wooded part
and then came out the other side, in the pasture which stretched
up to the crest of the hill and where cows were grazing.

You can imagine how we felt when the time came. Everybody
looked at their watches. And this was it. We joined hands. It was
like a pulse of electricity.

I said that each one of us had the same lofty idea. I don't mean
anything abstract. It was clear the purpose of the Great Chain
was to promote, to organize the sending of food to famine-
stricken areas. Not every American felt that way—the stirring of
generosity—only those who had taken the trouble to come out
on the line: 20 million of us. Perhaps 30 million—of every color
and description. What was most affecting, it was not only the
well-off and well-to-do; there were poor people here, whole fami-
lies on the line, who may well have gone hungry themselves and
skipped a meal. But what animated the whole thing, the entire
enterprise—and again, it involved millions—was not some ab-

stract idea but the picture in each person's mind, in the mind of the individual participant—you can say, the animating idea (of course seen in different ways and according to different temperaments and points of view, also depending on what they had witnessed in the newspapers or on television) of the recipient of the gift. The picture of some one person in Africa actually starving, a famine victim.

It's hard to tell just how it happened, that the Great Chain continued. Barbara and I were as surprised as anybody. We were better off than the others; we had brought a sleeping bag. Most came without any camping paraphernalia. Perhaps some brought picnic blankets or a hamper of food to last the family a day, or a poncho, and then decided in their enthusiasm to stay on. This was of course something the organizers had not anticipated. The organizers had a grand plan. They had been confident of their strategy, that it would catch on, that it would be a national event, and so forth, but had conceived of nothing beyond that. Not to say it was all media hype. It's just that the ordinary people on the line had gone beyond the organizers.

At the moment of closure, of joining hands, there were the TV cameras, the press, telegrams from governors. The big statement was being made. It had been made. And now it was the time for the personal statement.

As I say, Barbara and I were totally overwhelmed and so was everyone else. Here we were on the line making up the Chain. And so was everyone. Now that it had physically happened, it seemed so miraculous—the actual scene, the event, so impressive. I don't mean that, literally, they couldn't, or didn't, want to stop holding hands. Soon after the appointed time, people did that. People were strolling around, chatting, commenting on the Chain, stepping back to look at other segments of it. I suppose, to see if *that* part would hold. The line had become its own drama. So long as people could see themselves doing it, and see others not just giving way but holding the line, the spirit was there. In that sense the line was there, the Great Chain. The statement was being made. It was impossible not to continue making it.

We imagined the Chain reaching out across the valleys to our right and left, across the entire continent.

"It's holding!" I said. "It's really as long, as immense, as incredible as the Great Wall of China. A monument to spontaneity."

Barbara said, "It's America's affair of the heart."

2

We've been here a week. Tents have appeared at intervals along the route, in a variety of shapes and colors: blues, yellows, oranges. All very cheerful. When not manning the line, people stroll around listening to tape decks, are gathered in a circle cooking over Coleman stoves, or are off on some camp detail such as digging latrines.

We've run into some people we knew in Fort Wayne, in our church group. And we've made particular friends with another couple—their tent happened to be pitched next to ours. We met the first morning over breakfast. They go down to the river to fetch water, hand in hand.

Cecille is very quiet. She sits by the bank under a willow combing out her long blonde hair, while Otis whittles a tent peg. We've discovered that the four of us went to the same high school.

Otis has been telling us about the neighborhood he and Cecille live in in Fort Wayne. Their two families moved away. Could moving away to another place, and the estrangement involved, be the grounds for romance? Possibly.

When we were all in high school, Otis and Cecille didn't go around together, only dated occasionally. But later, after they had moved to this new place, they fell in love with each other and were married.

Mapledale is in another part of town, of Fort Wayne. Strangely enough Barbara and I have never been there. But it is basically just like Millwood, Otis says. Some things are different . . . details. There is a shopping center. A wide tree-lined avenue where the trolley car runs . . . a smaller center where there are a few stores and a restaurant, the *Idle Hour*. (We have an Idle Hour restaurant, too, in our neighborhood.) In the center a parking lot, at night people are always moving across it, getting in and out of cars. Streetlamps checkered by trees. Signs over the lighted store- fronts in rose, pink, lavender and blue. Blocks of lawns and houses. Single-car garages.

He describes Mapledale to us.
We wish we could go there.

Our valley is not far from Fort Wayne; that's convenient. It lies along the Sandy River, a tomato- and onion-producing region. So, of course we have onions and tomatoes and other farm produce. We've been going out, the four of us, in Barbara's Honda station wagon on food-foraging expeditions. There are farm produce stands on the roadside, and places where you can shop—hamlets or four-corner intersections where there is a filling station and convenience store.

The other day we stopped at a roadside stand beside a farm.

"But is this organic produce?" Barbara asked. She was at the stand buying corn.

"Everything here is natural," the farmer said. Some of his family had been standing with us on the line. We had come with our two friends, from the food provisioning detail.

"No chemical fertilizer? Only manure . . . and composting?"

"Manures of all kinds. Cows, sheep and goats, pigs . . . "

"I hear chicken manure is the best."

"For that you'll have to go up to the chicken farm." He pointed up the road. We had seen a large chicken farm about a mile up the highway. "It's a sight to see," the farmer went on. "Expanded several years ago. It's modernized. Totally mechanized. Everything packaged . . . frozen."

"Where do these chickens go?"

"Chicago, Minneapolis, New York, Boston. The slaughtered chickens fly everywhere."

"Are they shipped overseas?" Barbara asked. She was thinking of herself, personally, giving a starving person the chicken. Famine victims in Uganda, the Sudan, Tanzania.

"I believe that in Uganda," one of our friends (it was Otis) said, "starving peasants have their own food, certain kinds of grains. It has to be that or they won't eat anything. Their food is not our food."

We've been sitting around the Coleman stove telling about how we came here. In almost every case it was a mental image. Barbara had seen a photograph of squatters in the Philippines.

They were living in a section of Manila which was the city dump. Their shacks were on top of it (with many others). They lived by scavenging. The photograph showed the family out there picking over garbage on top of this mountain under a smoky sky . . . it was this image more than anything that stuck in Barbara's mind, and was responsible for her being here.

Otis had seen a picture of a sisal cutter in northeast Brazil. He was lying on the cracked earth of a field, with his machete thrown down before him, his two hands thrust out, as if he'd gone to sleep suddenly. He had a swollen belly. A beetle was crawling out of his mouth.

Cecille had seen a film of a refugee camp in the Sudan. The camera had caught a young woman on her way to the infirmary. In the background there were people (Sudanese? Ethiopians?) squatting on the ground in black robes; beyond the chain-link fence, a desert of sand. The woman—whom the camera had stopped on her way to the infirmary—had her head decorated with beads, and was holding to her breast the stick of a baby.

We had not shared any of these pictures before, though presumably many people on the Chain—perhaps millions—had the same mental images. In fact, they had been private, intensely personal experiences and we would not have thought of communicating them to anyone. It was as if, in some dark, secret room within us, they had now come to light. And we were sharing them because we were here out of respect for each other and because of our new sense of intimacy.

"I suppose *being* photographed, in those circumstances, must also be a private experience. For them," Cecille said. "It is their private experience, and our private experience."

Again she was seeing the mother holding the baby—which for all she (Cecille) knew might be dead—and wondering how she had woven her hair up like that, with little beads. Or was it cowrie shells or sections of bamboo?

3

It has taken enormous amounts of supplies to sustain the Great Chain, the Hunger Chain, that is, to keep it provided for, in being.

If the organizers had planned for, conceived of it lasting beyond the first day, no doubt they could have worked out the logistics. As it is, each section of the Chain has organized itself, has exercised the utmost ingenuity in provisioning its own members. It's lucky we're at the edge of the city with its shopping centers. On the other hand, the proximity of the city with its large populations adds to the size of the Chain, swells its numbers. And this requires more supplies: food, tents, gas for Coleman stoves, etc. (One cannot imagine the Chain passing by no large cities. They are necessary centers for information, fund raising, advocacy groups. Without them, it would not generate enough interest. It would not renew itself from week to week. It would become dispirited and run down.)

We've been visiting other sections of the Chain. This can be done driving along Highway 5. The road runs parallel to it. There is also a view of the farms, with the roofs of barns showing between the willows and locusts along the river. One is naturally curious. It's really interesting to keep in touch, to see how the rest of the Chain is doing, and keep abreast of events.

We have been making these excursions almost daily on food-gathering details, the four of us together. We've been using Barbara's Honda. Sometimes our own section furnishes us with a truck. Naturally everyone is involved in these duties. There is a sign-up sheet posted on the bulletin board. Here people can volunteer for various details: news and information, cleaning up the camp, recycling, and latrine digging. Of course provisioning and food gathering is the most important.

However, our own area is rapidly becoming exhausted; we have to go farther afield. The farms and roadside stands did a great business at first, everyone did well. It's always been convenient, when a section was out of something, for someone to drive in to one of the shopping centers. But the supply situation is getting pretty tight.

I run across Otis standing again in front of the bulletin board. I ask him why he signs up so often? Isn't it enough to go with us?

He was with the supply corps during the Vietnam War. He laughs. "I enjoy riding on trucks."

Cecille works as a lab assistant for the Food and Drug Administration in Fort Wayne. There are quite a few guitars in the camp. We hear them. Bluegrass. Folk. There are people in a group around them singing. Cecille has brought along her cello. She sits by herself, her head bent and hair falling forward, the instrument cradled between her knees.

I was surprised to hear, from Otis, that Cecille is suffering from a liver ailment, a condition that could prove fatal.

"But she is determined to stay on the line until the last hungry African is fed."

We have been to a picturesque rural cemetery, celebrating Armistice Day, the end of the war. It is high up, at the crest of the hill. From there we could see the Chain reaching out on both sides. It must stretch to the Atlantic Ocean. Along the western horizon there is smoke, murky haze, or anyway a great cloud hanging over the industrial city of Gary.

The cemetery is a touching spot, a grassed plot surrounded by a wrought iron fence. The crowd (many of the people from the Chain) press in among the graves, some small boys sitting on top of the burial vaults. Like the others, we have brought little American flags to place on the graves.

Now we are driving back. Cecille is in front, Otis driving. He says, "We have been burying the dead symbolically. Just as we are feeding the starving symbolically."

Cecille peers out into the dark through the windshield. Exhausted by the ceremony, she lays her head on Otis's shoulder.

We're stopping at the Idle Hour after dancing.

Cecille has become more and more concerned with helping the starving in Africa. She wishes she could do more. But realistically she cannot. This is all she can do, that is, to be faithful. She is only one person. And it is the *total*: the numbers of witnesses of conscience, persons making up the Chain. The fact that all these masses of people are holding hands is more than a symbol of this. It is in a sense a guarantee the food is on its way—of course through a host of intermediaries.

We were dancing earlier in the evening to the music of a small band whose members we met on Armistice Day. Two young men and a woman (the band is called "The Saints") all with fair hair, who took themselves so seriously as innovative composers they almost forgot to provide music you could dance to. There were times when you couldn't hear it at all.

From one of them we heard the rumor that certain segments of the Great Chain (it started with the three-state Iowa-Missouri-Kansas segment, and now it's moved to ours, Indiana and Illinois) are setting up special warehouses to furnish supplies. The trucks will be directed there. The job has simply become too big for a local supply depot.

Otis has heard this rumor, too. Tomorrow he is going out on a truck detail, and he may be able to find out about it.

"I still believe this, this whole thing," Otis says, "is being kicked up to a different scale—a higher and more centralized level—where spontaneity is no longer necessary. If not a national scale, at least a sub-national scale."

Cecille has had trouble sleeping. It may be her ailment. Or it could be the uneven ground of the tent. To comfort her we describe certain sections of Fort Wayne which she used to know as a girl, before her family moved away. Particularly our own section.

"It's pretty much the same as it was," we tell her. "Only some of the trees are taller."

We are planning to go dining again at the Idle Hour.

4

When they left the valley it was raining. Otis was on the truck with people he didn't know. "I really missed you and Cecille and Barbara." He was telling the story to us later.

As it turned out (Otis said), none of us had seen the place, the warehouse, before, the driver included. This was a new adventure for him, too. All we had was a map of how to get there. By this time there was a long line of trucks. They were all identical to our truck, all had the same markings. I was beginning to get the feeling of replication.

I figured we'd get our supplies all right and manage to get them to our home base, Sandy River. But there'd probably be long waits due to the number of trucks, maybe delays in getting our requisition order okayed by higher authorities and so forth. I remember these delays from the war. You're sent on these interminable trips. They're pointless and consist of nothing but these delays. But you enjoy them. It's boring, I guess. You have nothing else to do but look at the scenery. You're completely in the hands of fate.

Anyway, we were climbing, away from Sandy River, from the home base. And sure enough we arrived at this gate. The warehouse was not in sight. There was just this hill, and a chain-link fence going around the perimeter at the base. It was raining so you couldn't see anything. It must have been there, because there were trucks coming down fully loaded.

So we were at the gate. And sure enough, the line, which had been running pretty well up to this point, stopped for some reason. The truck in front of us was the last one through. We were stuck there.

I had a long conversation with the gatekeeper.

"You couldn't see the warehouse?" we asked him.

As I say, the road went up and disappeared in the fog. But this gatekeeper was interesting. A Czech or maybe a Bulgarian. He'd just come over to America. He answered this call from the employment agency. Here he was driving out to work every day from Fort Wayne. He spoke the language pretty well. Probably learned it from watching American movies.

"You say he was entertaining?"

We were stuck there for hours. Nothing to do but talk to him. He was a jovial enough fellow. He was short and stout—with a big handle-bar mustache—in his guard's uniform, loaded down with the accessories, belt, billy club, walkie-talkie.

"You asked him about the warehouse?"

As a matter of fact, he talked about the warehouse incessantly—which is pretty weird for a guard. Their minds are usually someplace else. These Middle- or East-European immigrants, they hire them and put them to work. And they have very backward notions about what goes on here.

"What was going on?"

Well, as far as I could see, it was just a warehouse. First of all, it must have been absolutely huge to handle the three-state area.

And because of the huge numbers of trucks. These Europeans don't understand scale. They're bowled over by it. The effect of the thing seemed to awe him.

"What do you mean by that?"

He saw it as a manifestation of power. Just because somebody owned it . . . they had *cornered* all that stuff . . . it was theirs. They had accumulated it, stolen it probably from all over the world. They'd locked it up and were going to sell it. That he took for granted. What impressed him was the power. He sensed it up there. It elicited his *respect*. For him there was this thing . . . the presence of the owners of the warehouse. They had a kind of baleful authority. He had a thoroughly archaic attitude. Almost medieval.

"A medieval attitude? The gatekeeper?"

I tried to point that out to him, tried to make him understand, that it's a question of scale, of logistics.

"You mean the warehouse?"

The warehouse is modern simply because of its size. In the old days such enormous size, simply the immensity, would have been inconceivable. And size is just a function. There are other functions . . . mathematical, algebraic, instrumental. It's hardly something physical at all. It's more like an operational formula. An exchange function.

"The guard didn't see this?"

Well, you couldn't see anything, literally. Because of the rain. All you could do was look up and wonder whether it was there. I'd say he didn't understand anything. He kept looking up at it in the rain . . . or rather, in that direction, and calling it "The Castle."

"The Castle? That's odd."

Kept referring to it as The Castle. "The Castle" . . . "Lord of the Castle" . . . "power relations" . . . "owners of the Castle." That kind of thing. He kept saluting and tipping his hat.

Cecille is telling me about her dream. "And you were in it."

"Was I?"

We are standing on the line, being part of the chain. Or perhaps we are at the Idle Hour.

"You were in the dream. You are in it."

In the dream (and it strikes me this is not a dream, it's something that may have happened. But if so, why is she telling it to me in this way?) . . . in Cecille's dream the truck is through the gate. We are all being taken up to the warehouse by the guard. It is early morning.

The guard or gatekeeper has become one of the men on a clean-up detail. They are wearing uniforms. Each has a cavernous bag slung from the waist and carries a pointed stick.

Now we are inside. A shaft of light illuminates the piles or heaps of grain which rise like hills to the girders. At the far end we can barely see a little rectangle of light from the further gate. A crew of clean-up men are moving on the piles of grain like ants. In between it is dark. A corridor or roadway runs along the center. On each side there are bins from which articles of food are collected. Behind these rise the heaps of loose grain to the roof.

The warehouse is over a railroad yard. Or over the docks. Somehow the city of Fort Wayne has been invaded by these docks, which are connected to the lake, from there through the Saint Lawrence Seaway to the ocean. The ocean cannot be seen, but it can be smelled. Beyond the corrugated metal walls are the cries of sea gulls.

A rumbling from below. At the far side of the warehouse a chain rising through a hole. This must be the hoist from a ship that is being unloaded. It swings out a cargo of bananas as tall as an apartment house.

Another group from the Chain—we recognize them from the encampment by the river—has been going through the series of bins, picking through the stacks of canned goods, barrels, and open sacks. These are thickly piled against the bulkhead which holds back the heaps and hills of loose grain.

We are climbing over a hill of millet. Other groups are also walking on the grain. There is a hillside of ground-nuts, and beyond a darker mound of coffee beans or cocoa. Cecille, dreaming, is reminded of climbing on the sand dunes by the lake shore. The waves and billows of the dunes seemed part of the lake itself, which had invaded the land, forming the wall of sand marking the edge of the forest and even drifting onto the highway.

Otis and I and Barbara are together. We have clambered up the slope, using our hands and feet to keep from slipping and sliding in the loose grain. Cecille reaches down. Her hands have uncovered a scrap of paper. It is a photo of a black woman bending down, a baby strapped to her back in a shawl. Bare to the waist. Her hair is beaded with strips of bamboo.

"It is the millet picker," Cecille tells Barbara.

Otis, going down the corridor shortly before, has discovered the portrait of an Indian woman in a sack of tea. It was like a cameo. Thin wrist with silver bracelet. The face almost hidden by the veil or sari. The large bright eyes outlined in collyrium dye.

Barbara on the next hill calls over to them and holds something up.

"Look what I've found. It's torn and dirty, but you can see."

"What is it?"

"The photo of a man cutting cane. These scraps of paper are everywhere."

"What do you think they are?" Otis says.

"These must be the harvesters or pickers," Cecille tells us. "Maybe these photographs are the way they identify themselves for the overseer . . . for the work they do, a kind of tally sheet. Or perhaps they're for us. They just wanted us to know who they are."

"They're everywhere."

We keep walking on the mounds. It is like clambering on the dunes. We keep slipping and sliding, picking up the photographs on the heaps of grain, like shells.

Now we have come up to the squad of maintenance men. The gatekeeper is explaining: "It's part of the job, guarding the warehouse, and also cleaning up the photos. They're dumped here, from the ships; it dirties the place up. Of course they can't just be left here for everyone to see. We have to pick them all out, with the sticks. They come in every night by the thousands. And by every morning we have to get rid of them."

■ Meeting Trains

There is hardly a perceptible line that one traverses in order to cross from the city into the suburbs. The brick industrial buildings and warehouses continued. I stood at a railroad crossing carrying a beat-up suitcase. A light was blinking and a bell was sounding monotonously. A passenger train which had been going slowly out of the central station was beginning to pick up speed. One of the conductors, standing on the steps, was just pulling the door shut. The windows were uniformly grimy; nothing could be seen inside but a vague blur. But one of them was open and a young woman in a red scarf was leaning out. Her face had an expression of happiness from the air rushing against her face. As she saw me she waved.

The bell stopped ringing and the gate went up.

My impression was that I had been standing in a crowd of pedestrians and bicycles. Now I was walking on alone.

I was in a cafeteria talking to two men. I told them I had come to look for a relative of mine, McTeague. "You'll never find him," one of them told me.

The other said, "Around here almost everyone is a McTeague. And they all come from Twin Forks, Nebraska."

When I had first come to the suburbs some weeks ago, I boarded in a house run by a family of that name. They lived on a street of single- and two-family houses, with elm trees, and sometimes a Model A Ford parked in front.

This family has two children, boys, who are always playing in the street. The man, Slim, has a forbidding expression. He is away from the house all day. When he returns, I'm made uncomfortable. We gather around the dining table and eat supper in absolute silence, looking down at our plates, the wife standing behind the husband's chair.

I take this to be the custom of country people.

I've been spending the day at the cafeteria with my two friends, Bowler and Stump. They also live in rooming houses, are about the same age as myself, with the same degree of baldness. No matter what the weather, Bowler sits in the cafeteria in an overcoat much too large for him, with a once-fashionable beaver collar. He removes his hat only to scratch his head or to wipe his forehead with a soiled bandanna. He describes how he got the overcoat. Arriving here from the foothills of Arkansas, petrified by the cold, he stole it from a stiff in a boxcar. He thought the man was already frozen. The story fills him with joy.

Stump was a journeyman carriage maker and had worked many places, among them Baldwin locomotive works, where he had lost three fingers. He would hold out his hand to me, showing the missing fingers, and laugh.

The cafeteria is a refuge for homeless men. What else is there to do there except tell stories?

I'm telling about my own life in the inner city, overwhelmed by garish lights. They listen. After all, our pasts are not unlike each other. My own story, which I feel ebbing away from me like a slack tide in the cafeteria, is the same as theirs. As I speak of what I have left behind—of love, pain, and unsatisfactory relationships—I feel my face flush and my eyes begin to fill with tears.

The head of the household, McTeague, is not given to effusive speech. I'm told by Anna McTeague they were hoping to have more roomers, to add to the family income, but that had not worked out. They seem to have enough money for what Anna calls "the conveniences"—by which she means her washing machine and a Singer sewing machine, the prize possession of the house.

I stand behind Anna, not five feet away, while she is vacuuming the parlor rug. She wears a flowered print dress, open at the neck and upper arms to give her room to maneuver. There is the smell of bread from the kitchen.

Anna doesn't share her husband's anxieties about the children. If there are dangers of unforeseen adventures on the city streets, they will be up to dealing with them.

"The children go anywhere."

She tells me a story about an adjacent neighborhood. It is older than this one. Perhaps I had seen it as I walked through. It seems these people are from a certain province in northern India where they were weavers.

"You won't believe this . . . This section is called a Katha-kali. And the most amazing thing about it is, all the men are missing a hand."

"All of them?" This strikes me as a naive exaggeration.

"No. I'm not joking. They were weavers. The way things were, they had a handloom set up in the house. It was hot and damp so they worked under an awning on the roof where there was air. Or in a courtyard. The weavers were men. They're the ones who make clothes. Anyway, there were laws against competing with the British goods that were being shipped in. They were not allowed to weave cloth. And when they did . . . *this* was done to them. Just like that."

Anna makes a stiff gesture over her wrist and shudders.

The cafeteria is at a crossroads between several sections of the suburb. Here the trolley lines come through. There is a movie house and some stores. Next to the cafeteria is a cafe, what Jamaicans call a "grog shop." From here the Jamaican cane cutters come in smelling of rum.

We and the other regulars were amazed at these cane cutters. They were enormous blacks. Others were Haitian or Dominican, usually slender men, with not the strength of the blacks, smaller and more wiry. But they were ferocious operators. And more than once in the dingy monotone of the cafeteria there would be a demonstration of how to cut cane.

There were no real machetes. This was a demonstration in the technique of how to cut cane: stance, stroke of the blade, resist-

ance of the cane, which was like a wall. So that to cut it was a
fight, and cane cutters with shouts advanced on it as upon the
enemy in battle—the heat, the fuzz, the dust from the cane get-
ting in their eyes. It was fierce work. But their pride seemed
equally fierce and terrible.

Actually they had no tools; they had left them behind. This
was harvest in their imagination. But such was the energy, the
expressive quality of the demonstration in the art of cane cut-
ting, that after the men had gone and we were at the table over
our coffee dishes, we thought we had seen the slash and stab of
their machetes.

"And did you make a living at it?" Bowler asked.

Stump asked, "Did you ever go hungry?"

They spoke of the Dead Season. This was the season between
crops on the plantations when there was no work, when the
children had swollen bellies. The large families looked to the
man to bring food.

"La morte saison," a big black man would say to me, with a
grimace, looking me straight in the eyes. "And that's no phrase in
a song either. People become as lean as the wind."

We were sitting at the cafeteria window. We watched Mc-
Teague go by. Where does he work? That was something each of
us wondered about.

He stopped in front of us. He was very tall with stooped
shoulders, arms remarkably long, ending in raw, empty fists.

I understood in Nebraska he had been a farmhand. He drove
teams of horses on a big wheat farm. There would be four to a
dozen teams of Belgians, harnessed together, moving over the
hillside in a diagonal line, pulling the plow through the black
earth. Slim at the head shouting, holding the lead rein, his feet
also plunging in the muddy earth.

Now he seemed aimless, almost incapable of movement.

Moving indifferently down the street he had stopped just at
the edge of our line of vision. We could see him staring at his
reflection in the store window.

Such was the rule of silence at mealtimes, such was the accepted monotony of life at the McTeagues, that I was surprised when one evening Anna announced that tomorrow we were going to a "social."

The social was to be a husking bee. As we walked down the tree-lined street, we were joined by other families from the Twin Forks neighborhood. Anna became talkative. She had already started "visiting."

The barn, which could be seen from the street, was behind two houses. There was a backyard, a gravel drive going through it. Across this space swarms of neighborhood children were playing "kick the can," heckled by squawking geese.

The husking began. The plank floor of the barn was cleared. Around the pile were arranged benches. You reached forward and stripped out an ear. The hoard of greenish husks were thrown in back of the bench—they would be used for pigs. The pile at the center of the circle rose higher and higher, till it reached over our heads and grew yellower and shinier.

The women had become animated by the event, by the gossiping and flying fingers. The men stood outside the circle watching noncommittally. There was some drinking going on. There would be more liquor and fights.

There was the sound of fiddle scraping. Soon the husking bee would be transformed into a square dance.

The tradition of the social had begun for these scattered families living miles away, and needing a break in their isolation after the long months between harvests.

As I shucked corn, I imagined over my head a huge expanse of sky.

Now couples were dancing. There was the smell of the sweet green corn mixed with the dancers' and huskers' sweat.

I looked up. Through the door of the barn I saw a wagon moving by, bringing several more farm families. It stopped and they clambered down stiffly, swinging their arms in the cold. They must have come from a distance. The women's bonnets and shawls were covered with dust.

The cafeteria is a kind of limbo. The night before I was sitting in a far corner. There were few customers. A busboy was wiping tables with a rag. By the counter, with its polished surfaces, a waitress was having a cup of coffee and a cigarette with the dishwasher. In the dimness of the room, this area was brightly lighted, like a stage. Suddenly the cafeteria filled. A movie had let out. There was a river as if let loose from the street of jostling and shambling men. They were moving in a line in front of the serving counter. I watched Bowler and Stump. As they came toward me with their trays, it seemed to me I could see through them, as if they were transparent.

Today we have our regular seat by the window. What stories are there left to tell?

Again Bowler solemnly removes his hat, rests it on the table, and stares into its emptiness. Stump is affectionately considering his hand, with the lost fingers. He has been rearranging piles of coins.

Perhaps we're waiting for the ritual of McTeague passing in the direction of the railroad station.

He passes. There is endless curiosity about this.

"Where do you think he's going? Looking for a job?"

"Maybe he's fucking off someplace. Drinking."

"Has he got some woman?"

"There aren't any women."

"Has he got some job on the sly and hasn't told us?"

"If there is a job, how did he get it? Why should it be McTeague who is working when no one else is?"

I realize that behind all this there is intense envy.

Each neighborhood is called by a different name in a different language. We've been told that in the next neighborhood they bake bread and distribute it in baskets on their heads. Also there are cows inside the city. Since the suburbs are on a slope (they ring the city on all sides to the horizon), the river is at the bottom. The cows are driven down the streets by boys sitting on their backs. Milk is sold every morning by young women on horseback who go from house to house, the cans strapped to either side.

In the sky on certain nights south and west we can see fireworks. This is their Festival of Five Kings. They parade through the streets with elaborate floats.

Fireworks in the sky. An explosion of colored lights. Is this the same sky as the one, cold, limitless and blue, over our own neighborhood?

Outside the cafeteria window the traffic circle was obscured and the air dimmed with snow. There was the glow of traffic lights and the neon signs showed a garish pink. Though the snow fell, it did not last and the pavements were slick.

Under a lamp post a Salvation Army band was playing. They were three women and two middle-aged men. They were in uniform. The women, with raw faces and red, chapped hands, were wearing bonnets and capes. They were playing brass instruments. One of the men was seated at an out-of-tune piano that had been brought in a truck.

The sturdy country women made me think of Anna. But they had a dispirited and lifeless quality. It was as if, at the same time as they resisted the city, they were absorbed and defeated by it.

Still, there was a determined quality, with the black and scarlet of the uniforms, and gold braid, and the way the large man supported the tuba on his shoulder. But the uniforms were too stiff, the frozen fingers barely moved. The instruments seemed to be playing mechanically as if by themselves.

It was the perfect music for aimless men.

We were following Slim. He was slouched over, his hands in his pockets, the coat collar turned up. He had gone past a line of second-hand stores along the trolley line toward the section called "Mexico."

The railroad station which serves this section of the city is also called Mexico.

McTeague disappeared into a lunchroom opposite the station. Through the window we could see him sitting at the table reading the paper. We went in.

"How you doing, Slim?"

"What have you been up to?"

"How's the world treating you?"

He told us he was having a cup of coffee before going to work. He was a porter at the railroad station.

Bowler and Stump were looking in that direction.

"Would there be any more porters' jobs?"

"No. They're all filled. And besides, these passengers don't have a helluva lot of baggage."

"So, this is where you hang out mostly?" Stump asked.

McTeague had on his porter's uniform.

The station was on the far side of a large square. There were statues occupied by pigeons and some paths between bare ground. A trolley coasted up under the overhang along the station, which had an old-fashioned tower, and pulled away.

We were inside the station. The pavement was marked in squares. It was an old, very large building. Columns rose up, but the ceiling could not be viewed, it was obscured by scaffolding. Large areas of the pavement below were covered by a painter's dropcloth. From the round window under the tower rays of sunlight slanted down.

At first the station seemed empty. Then as one got used to the dimness, one could see that a part of it, probably the waiting room section with its long benches, was entirely occupied. The benches were filled with sleepers, whole families seemed to be camped on the floor. The light from the window, descending in a dusty pathway, fell on a great clock. And beside it onto an iron-framed bulletin board giving the arrival times of trains. Only ARRIVALS were marked. There were no Departures.

We sat for what seemed a long time with Slim, at the edge of the section of sleepers, the only sound being the movement of the other porters as they pushed their baggage carts, the complaint of the iron wheels. And far up somewhere under the scaffolding the drowsy murmur of pigeons. From time to time a child cried, or someone would cross to the information desk. They would be enquiring, Slim told us, about a friend or relative due to arrive from their own village.

"They are arriving out of the past," McTeague said.

We recognized one of the cane cutters.

The arrival of a train was being announced over the loudspeaker. We were moving with McTeague over the floor, his shoulders hunched over his handcart. We were temporarily halted before a gate, and here we had a few moments to wait in an area which was cramped, cold, and gloomy. Then we were through and onto the platform. At the very moment when the train was easing to a stop. The bulk of the engine high above us, its wheels making their last revolution, the gleaming pistons their last thrust. From underneath a burst of steam escaped and flew up to the roof girders of the shed. The entire roof of the great shed was filled with steam. But at the far edge we could see the countryside. Which was in fact clear to the eye. It was completely illuminated, as it stretched out on a slight rise all the way to the horizon.

McTeague had now reached the far end of the platform; we could still make out his uniform. But we were beginning to lose him among all the others—or we were about to lose him among the mass of new arrivals. The train had come to a halt, the car doors pushed open. Passengers were descending the steps with their baggage. Already they were beginning to stream down the platform in the direction of "Mexico."

TWO

In the Air

■■■ In the Air

1

There's an airstrip in our backyard. They say that it's ours. But we have no title to it and only recently found out it was there. It's not a small airstrip. It's in an open field, in a part of the property which was once farmed but had grown up to brush. You could call it a hidden airstrip. All these former meadows were bounded by stone walls along which trees and bushes have grown up over a period of time. They were each reached by a lane for wagons. And the road to the airstrip is still usable. In fact it passes right by our house.

The airstrip is there. But we have never seen any of the airplanes. We hear the noise all the time. When the pilots take off they make no attempt to hide the noise, how could they? A deafening sound. It's as if the whole sky directly over the house were being torn apart and exploding. Then the plane is gone, impossible to tell in what direction. This thundering sound is heard all over town. The noise is acceptable because it's self-evident. It's simply there. So it's not like it's some clandestine operation and anyone is trying to conceal it for some wicked or illegal purpose. The noise is there. Everyone hears it and understands it. That is its protection.

Still, the airfield is used night and day. So in a sense it's a regular operation. There's no mystery about what planes are being flown. They don't all have the same sound; they have many different ones. So people have become expert in listening.

This is particularly true of the high school boys who, from the noise, can tell what plane is being flown, its type, even with a fair degree of accuracy its engine make. Sometimes they can even tell whether it is a new model or an old one.

There are constant flights with this excruciating and terrifying noise. By now everyone has accepted it. Some people even welcome it as a sign of the town's prosperity. This is the claim of the mayor and the city council. Since the noise is so large, there must be something happening. People are drawn from all over. The streets are full of airmen. With all this, you'd think people would trust it, the airfield. But after all, it was hidden for a long time, kept secret. But why? This in itself makes it suspicious.

2

The school children have identified a new plane. This happened, positively, on a certain day. They were on their way to school. There was the noise of aircraft passing overhead, a common feature of the early morning hours when people are going to work and the children to school. One of them halted on the sidewalk, his head tilted back. Of course, the others stopped too. The boy's body was stretched taut and his eyes half closed, as if this posture afforded the maximum degree of discrimination and as if summoning the intelligence to bear. The noise was not quite the same as before. It was fractionally different, perhaps a shade more treble.

"It's an OV1 Mohawk."

This was the conclusion of the others, the rest of the students. And soon was the opinion of the rest of the town.

The new plane being flown out of the airstrip is a certain military reconnaissance plane. All the planes are new, they have this new sound. The old sound had been produced by combat planes. But these are reconnaissance and observation planes: the sound is softer and gentler. Now it is quite clear to everyone why the airstrip had been concealed. Even the authorities admit it. Before, if you asked them about it, they would deny there was an airstrip. But then there would be this terrifying noise. So the flying activity was obvious. Previously the pilots had operated in hostile territory against a distant enemy. They had claimed they were commercial pilots. This, far from being a lie, was an elaborate cover in order to protect the airstrip. Perfectly legitimate as it turned out, or at least necessary.

Now everyone knows what is happening and this is a great relief to everyone. The war is over—or at least everyone assumed there has been a war. This is especially a relief to the young men, the flyers, who are now allowed to be truthful. They have always been admired. People like to see them strolling down the street in their uniforms arm in arm with the young women.

Now they are engaged in testing or training flights. And what they are testing, what they are training for, are these OV1 Mohawks.

This plane is of an advanced type. It is of the latest design. Everyone is talking about it and is interested in it. You'd think the pilots would have been resentful of the students for identifying the secret plane from its sound. At first they had belittled the discovery. And even tried to confuse them, the children, by saying that the sound came from a different kind of observation plane, a C130 Hercules with a turbo-prop engine. But now the pilots are even pleased that everyone knows about the plane, or wants to know, in all its details. There has even begun a public lecture series at the local high school, conducted by the pilots (many of whom are graduates) in which we are taught about the plane: its state-of-the-art propulsion, its fuel-injection systems, its advanced telecommunication and instrumentation, its highly sophisticated information- and data-gathering systems. The capabilities of the plane have charmed everyone.

3

The children have gotten to know one of the airmen. This happened during the school lectures. This man is a technician, not a pilot. At the lectures it's the pilots who do all the talking. It may be because of the military hierarchy. As a technician he's obligated to be there and back the pilots up in case there are questions, but not talk. During the lectures he falls asleep. He sits up in the seat straight with his eyes blinking, then begins to nod. There are deep circles around his eyes like an owl.

Perhaps we've become friendly with him because of his sleepiness. In any case the children have made friends with Agnus. Often they've brought him home to the farm. He likes it here and seems to belong here.

That's probably because he's lonely. The base has grown much larger. The air force barracks are crowded; there's no privacy. It must be hard for people like Agnus who come from a farm background and have a solitary nature. He's from the Ozarks. Not even a young man. He must be in his mid-thirties. Sometimes he looks older, with his deep, sad eyes that have a simple gaze, and with cheeks sagging from chewing tobacco. So it's not surprising that, having been welcomed here, he should want to stay here. He enjoys helping with chores. Sometimes he sleeps over, sharing a room with the boys. This doesn't happen often. He flies at night, but sometimes he comes here directly from the airfield, and goes upstairs. You find him stretched out asleep on one of the boys' beds.

People have come from the neighborhood to watch Agnus. Not that there's anything special about him. He's a farmer like the rest of us. People watch him doing chores around the barn, carrying buckets of water, giving the pigs their feed, throwing scraps to the ducks. The same things that all of them do every day, and which have become even boring. But they wonder about Agnus. People will be at the store and they'll ask, "Did you hear the planes being tested last night?" And in the same breath, "Did Agnus stay over at the base, or has he come home?" If the answer is that he is home, the whole neighborhood will want to come over and see him.

It's as if the children had discovered their own airman. As if he dropped down on them from the sky. People will even climb up the back stairs to peek in at him sleeping on the bed. Exhausted from his night flight, in his sweaty undershirt—mechanic's overalls and huge boots on the floor, lying on his back with his mouth open.

Still, there are questions about Agnus. What does he do exactly? We know that he's a communications operator of some sort. But what does he communicate? And if this is an observation plane, what does it observe?

Before, they concealed the airport from us, and even concealed the war. Now we have this base. They say it's for training, and for observation and reconnaissance planes. But people are skeptical. They pulled the wool over our eyes once before. Why wouldn't they do it again?

We were behind the barn with Agnus. The neighborhood had gathered to watch him pluck chickens.

The women had a big barrel of boiling water. They were sticking them in the water to soften them, and then plucking them. Damp feathers were everywhere. There was a pile of feathers up to everyone's knees.

"Look at him," some of the men were saying. "Agnus, you're really going right to it."

"Agnus, how come you're such an expert chicken plucker? I thought you only liked to hunt with a coon dog."

The men enjoyed kidding Agnus. Agnus was tired and his eyes looked bloodshot. With his large mournful eyes, drooping lids, and the bottom of his cheeks sunken, he looked something like a hound.

"The trouble with you is, you don't get enough sleep. You do too much of this night flying," some of the men were saying.

One of the children said, "We don't even believe there is a plane."

Of course, this wasn't true. We'd heard some people, the mayor and some people who had pull with the pilots, had already been taken on a tour, on some of the training flights.

One of the children said, "Yes, we heard about that. Agnus, why don't you take us with you? Then we could see the plane."

Agnus doesn't like to talk, and when he does it's real gentle and slow. We were standing in a circle around him, close enough to hear what he said, but far enough away to be out of range of his spitting tobacco.

"Aw, come on, Agnus. Why don't you take us all up?"

Agnus shifted his feet uncomfortably and wiped some moist feathers off his hands.

"I don't know if I could," he said in a low voice, as we strained to catch it. "God, I don't fly the plane, I'm just up there."

We told him, "Agnus, you may not fly the plane. But you're a flyer!"

4

We were all crowded into the plane. It seemed the whole town was there. From the airport runway it had the appearance of just a small plane—an ordinary OV1 Mohawk Reconnaissance or the slightly larger C130 Hercules. But once inside—some of us pressed against the walls and some sitting or lying on the floor— the plane seemed to enlarge itself, to stretch itself as if designed to accommodate large numbers.

The farmers had just come from their evening chores, their boots coated with chicken manure. The pilots were wearing their fatigue uniforms. They joked with the passengers as they filed in, and looked unkempt and untidy.

But once airborne all this changed. The plane lightened itself, became something not of tremendous bulk, but fragile. The engine sound steadily moving ahead, not at great speed, sometimes the plane dipping and sliding sideways in the airflow. We had the feeling of cruising on a boat. Each passenger had a window or porthole. We were peering into an ocean of darkness—as if following a distant coastline.

We heard the phrase: "Running without lights" . . . and the words, "patrol . . . evasive action," coming from the flight cabin. We wondered at this—since it was a training flight, or at most a reconnaissance flight—and what it was that was being patrolled. But we refrained from asking, not wishing to disturb the smoothness of the flight and the steady hum of the engine.

However, one of the pilots said over the intercom: "We're over the sea. You can observe it, as you look out of the porthole, by its faint luminosity. Soon we'll be passing over the jungle, you'll be able to smell it."

In a moment we dipped down. The sea sheen disappeared, and there was the unmistakable smell of humid earth and vegetation.

"We're passing through the airspace of a friendly country. We are observing—soon we'll be observing—hostile elements. We'll be making a reconnaissance of them."

The other pilot said, "We welcome you aboard. When you feel cramped, feel free to get up, stretch your legs. You can have a cup of coffee at the machine. We make this same run every night; we call it the Milk Run. We have to cover the same territory over and over. So it gets boring, the novelty wears off. That's why we like to have passengers on board."

And again there was the weight on us of the cabin's darkness and the monotonous droning of the engine.

At first there had been the hidden airstrip. That was because there was a hidden war. Then there had been the time when everyone was admiring the test plane and studying its capabilities, talking about it and speculating about it. But no one had ever seen it, because it operated only at night. And now we were being taken up on one of these night flights.

Only a few feet separated the pilots from Agnus. He was crouched at the center of the hull or shell, his upper body and shoulders thickened by a flack jacket and his head masked by earphones. In front of him and to the side was a monitoring screen and amplifiers. We imagined Agnus listening intently through these, and observing what could be seen with his owl's eyes, which in the night had grown larger.

But in fact not much was coming through. All was quiet, except for a faint static. Agnus, positioned before the bank of instruments, his hands resting on the switches and dials, seemed not so much operating them as merely connected to them, in phase with them. The instruments themselves, though a small part of the plane—and though at the moment they were registering nothing—seemed to be registering the heartbeat of the flight, hours passing of the night, and the motion of the plane through the sky.

The two pilots sat with their backs to us before a wall of instruments and lighted dials, and were peering—like Agnus— through some aperture into darkness. They were separated by a narrow space. From behind, one could only see the edges of the two bodies. A hand rested gently on a knee. Or every so often, on impulse, would reach over into the other pilot's space and flick a switch or pull down a lever.

We strained to listen. But if there was anything to hear it was within the closed circuit of Agnus's headset. The screen was blank.

Then on the monitoring screen there were blips of radar,

blooming, coalescing, and vanishing. The static became more insistent. We leaned forward in our seats.

The reconnaissance plane was far above the earth but tied to it remotely—like a spider floating in the air, suspended from a thread. There was nothing that could be hidden. The instruments extended our own eyes and ears. Through the reach of darkness, the monitoring and sensing devices were registering what was happening on the ground far below, under the leaves: the cries of birds . . . the pressure on a twig of animals and men. Their secret movements along the paths, their whispered conversation, even breathing.

We would have liked to ask Agnus what the signals meant. But we were behind him. The air in the cabin was too thick. There were too many of us for our voices to reach him.

MORAZÁN

You, Sebastian, have slept all night on the bus. A night ride over the mountains from San Salvador. You're a long way from the coast, from the tall office buildings. You're headed for the countryside.

Daylight.

The province of Morazán.

Behind you the kingdom of hawks and condors, whose wings glide with the slopes of volcanoes. Suddenly the ground plunges. A green wall of *ceiba*, oak, *cocanaste*, tall feathering trees strung with lianas, vines spiraling up. And occasionally a gully, a red gash of earth torn in the bank. The woods close in. You see the first signs of settlement, a man driving a donkey loaded with firewood. The bus swerves and shudders. It's full of peasants picked up at the last stop.

Now you're on the flat. The road has leveled out, traveling between the fields. This is a country of farms. Level fields low to the river, the *Quebrada El Mozote*. You don't have to be standing beside the river, Sebastian, to know it's dry. You went here when you were a little boy. You bathed here, and watched the washer women, their legs slick. They were beating clothes against a rock, calling to one another.

Memories of childhood.

Sebastian, how you loved to be taken on the backs of these women.

The bus window is grimy. On one side there are farms. Squares and rectangles of cotton, maize, beans. Further up, the bare fields, *pastos*, for grazing cattle, and the darker slopes of coffee. Beyond, the forest you've just come through. Rolling out behind the bus a banner of dust. Between borders of spiky trees, the road runs in an absolutely straight line.

A full busload. On the seat across from you, two peasants. You think they may be returning from a refugee camp from the look of them. A lined old woman and a red-faced young man who could be her grandson. The man with calloused hands, feet awkwardly straddling a crate; between the slats beady-eyed chickens. The old lady is hugging in her lap a bulging corn sack. She reaches in (you smile because this gesture is familiar to you), pulls up a handful of grain. And without thinking, without looking at them, with the fingers rubs over them, like telling a rosary.

Something has happened, the bus is slowing down. You, Sebastian—who are a Salvadoran through and through— expected this. After all, this is your country. The bus has come to a stop before a line of soldiers, a brown-green camou- flaged *mazinger* personnel carrier parked under some trees.

Roadblock.

Passengers are moving to the front. Driver sits with his cap pushed back, hands resting on the wheel, passively. Soldiers have ordered everybody out. You're moving forward, seeing through the lower half of the window the feet, black boots of the *guardia* straddled on the pavement, leather silver-studded belt and pistol holder. The inside of the bus is like a furnace.

You're not worried. A hassle. But your I.D. card is in order. You don't look at them, the soldiers. Naturally you're delighted to do whatever they tell you to. You step down from the bus, shielding your eyes from the sun's glare and join the line of men facing against the bus, their feet spread apart, to be searched. Hands stretched up, leaning forward against the burning me- tal, you turn your head to watch the two peasants stepping out of the bus after you, under the eyes of the *guardia*.

* * *

Now the bus is moving forward again. You, Sebastian, are listening to your Walkman, plugged to your ears. (Michael Jackson, you enjoy the latest hit tunes from the U.S.) Approaching town, you look out the window and see the peasants leaving for the countryside. This happens every day. In the day they go out to tend their fields, they work. And at night, come back to town to sleep, or listen to the bombing.

What you're looking at of course is a countryside which has been systematically wrecked, hardly a stretch of cornfield or barley without a bomb crater in it. And if you could see them (beyond the orchards of mangoes and lemons— themselves torn and strafed) the hamlets where these farmers once lived, obliterated . . . La Joya, El Mozote. Nothing left but a jagged wall, maybe a hammock strung between two trees. Villages, Sebastian, you used to know well.

The planes cruise in from Illopango, the base from which they call in the air strikes. But they have the generosity to bomb the countryside at night. In the daytime it's left alone. The town is spared. One of the accommodations, the little delicacies of war. In El Salvador everyone understands everything.

The farm workers are going out. You're watching them carrying their machetes to turn the soil by hand. Or a *huizote*, a mattock on their shoulders for the steep slopes. The men with their heads and feet the color of leather, in white cotton trousers tied at the knees. The women bareheaded with black braided hair, or with colored scarves.

And this puts you in mind of the grandmother and the young man. At the last roadblock. Nothing can keep a peasant in the camps. They make difficulties for them of course. They return—but it's forbidden to plant seed, to bring extra food. Still, all they want to do is return to their land, their *petate*.

You see them in your mind's eye, moving down the aisle at the command of the soldiers. What are they thinking? The old lady clutching her sack. The boy or young man, smarter, leaving his crate under the seat. But probably worried it will get stolen. The woman on the top step with her black dress and thin wrists (you watch, your feet straddled, your hands raised against the metal) the grandson close behind but not touching her or helping her. Their faces tell you nothing. But her step betrays her. Her foot freezes . . . refuses to seek ground, to leave the sanctuary of the bus. The *guardia* with their fingers on their guns and their hard eyes, watching from five feet away.

Then the heap of corn dumped on the ground burning. It flares up in a blaze. The soldiers have taken the man up the road in the direction of the mazinger. You hear a shot. And the old woman screaming.

* * *

Now the bus is entering town. You'll be glad, Sebastian, to be climbing down at the plaza by the newspaper kiosk.

A long night, the ride over the mountains. And now the first shade. Narrow streets. The stucco amber- and lavender-tinted walls, a barred window and a sign nailed up. An attractive face peers down: advertising the soft drink FANTA.

A war against the peasants.

They come back. The peasant always comes back to the bombed-out fields, the shredded orchards. And they know the price paid for everything. They don't fool themselves.

The roadblock.

It's all behind you: the little heap of corn smoking. The empty road, the form sunk on the asphalt. Nothing but the glare of the sun. The witnesses.

You can imagine how it is. You know them. First they were in the fields beyond the hedgerow; they heard the shots. But they waited till it was safe, till they heard the sound of the mazinger taking off down the road. Then they came to look.

Of course there's nothing to surprise them. In your mind's eye you see them, Sebastian. A few adults, the rest children. They're standing in a half circle; the sun's beating down. In the sun's glare it's all clear to them.

A woman is pointing down, going over perhaps how it happened, for the girl beside her who hardly comes to her waist. The little girl in a pink dress, her hands clasped at her throat.

And looking off somewhere . . . at the trees, as if listening to
a bird. She's not thinking about something. The little boy
also barefoot. His feet planted solidly on the ground. His
arms crossed. Staring down at the corpse, gravely studying it.

5

"We've picked up the guerrillas," one of the pilots said. "We've
made contact. We've picked up their walkie-talkies."

"We're observing them," the other pilot said. "We are only mon-
itoring them, we don't intend to hurt them. Anyway, they may
not even be down there. They may be all dead, or operating in
another part of the country."

We wondered what country we were flying over.

Agnus, in a gesture of relief at having contacted the guerrillas,
pushed back the headset and stuffed into his mouth a chew of
tobacco. He leaned back. We had noticed, as we filed into the
plane, a photograph taped up beside him: from the Ozarks, his
family clustered around a hound dog.

There was something mesmerizing in the shifting configura-
tions on the panels which made us sleepy. Or perhaps it was that,
because of the number of passengers, the air was being used up.
The system operated independent of the pilots, independent of
us. It went on gathering information, whatever its objective. And
would go on.

The pilots seldom moved except for the minute play of criss-
crossing hands. It was as if the two men were tied together. They
rested in their seats without stirring, except when the plane
descended or elevated to a new flight level. It was as if the flight
could go on forever.

And so we were surprised when one of the pilots turned to us
and said, "Well, that about wraps it up. We'll make a last run over
the area and then head home."

We wondered what we had seen. It was impossible to ask Ag-
nus. Sprawled in his seat, his back sharply arched, his knees
tightly drawn up before him and pushing against the monitoring
screen, his face was toward us. But the eyes were hidden behind
the heavy lids. He could have been peering at the monitoring
screen.

The other pilot said, "If you're thinking about the meaning of the information, that doesn't concern us. We just collect it. It takes about two hours for the information to reach where it is going. There is a hookup to Panama, and from there it's transmitted to a hookup in a certain room in the Pentagon where the data is interpreted. And from there it is sent by *telex* back to an air base in this country where we are now."

"What is the country?" we asked him.

"I couldn't tell you if I knew. The name of the base is Illopango, but it's probably just a code name to identify the friendly country. We could just as well be on another flight over another country. The OV1 Mohawk would perform just the same.

"Well, that about wraps it up. We'll be heading back now. While we've been turning the plane, the sun has come up. You may have noticed it. We'll make one more pass in daylight. We'll be flying low over the countryside, so you'll be able to see it."

Now the dawn light, like some liquid whiteness, filtered into the interior of the plane, slowly soaking it. Our faces looked drained. The interior of the plane, crowded with townspeople, was like a bus which had journeyed through the night, cluttered and dirty.

After losing our bodies to the darkness and to the flight, we could begin to see each other.

The windows had grown transparent.

We were rubbing our eyes, trying to get the grit of darkness out of them.

Outside it was full daylight.

We had come in over the treetops, flying low. The river meandered peacefully through the farming valley, whose fields were cut into small patches by trees. The mountains were beyond, on one side dark, on the other light in the morning sun.

The river, wandering through the farmland, was a bright mirror which at intervals reflected the shadow of the plane, as we passed over it in a straight line.

We could see every blade of grass.

We saw nothing.

■ Reading the Meter

1

One day the meter-reading man came from Southern Vermont
Public Service. He drives a company pickup truck in all seasons.
Goss sees him clumping across the yard, head down, in the direc-
tion of the utility pole. Or has a glimpse of his back as he retreats
from the scene, having completed the job of meter reading, the
orange and blue pickup disappearing around the curve.

These visits would be even less an event if the customer were
living in town. The electricity meter would be at the base of the
house a foot from the sidewalk. The meter man would routinely
check it, and never be seen. As it is, Goss's house is isolated. It is
a quarter mile up the road, which runs beside a hay field and
through the pine woods. The line was run fifty years ago in
Goss's father's time. Now the right-of-way must be kept open at
great inconvenience to the company. The brush must be cut
down, etc.

It is probably this distance through the woods, and the fact
that very often Goss doesn't see him (the man does the job quick-
ly—parking the truck at the end of the drive, leaps out and
crosses the yard toward the pole) that makes these visits some-
what mysterious. Of course, reading the meter leaves no trace.
There is no way of knowing when he's been here, except when
there are tracks in the snow or on rare occasions when there is
mud. Maybe Goss goes to the edge of the yard where the high
grass has been trodden down, or there is an early morning
dew . . . there are footprints leading to the pole. And so these
visits have a furtive and secretive quality.

One morning Goss received an electricity bill. Besides the

usual sheet of paper giving the bill period—June 15th to July 15th
and the rate—there was an additional item.

8 people killed in the village of Jinoteca Nicaragua.
Externalities $31.00

followed by the explanation:

This amount is usually deducted from your ongoing credit
account and does not normally appear in billing.

This seemed more than a bookkeeping error. The bill, of
course, was made up mechanically in the accounting department
and beyond human intelligence. One could not hold the compu-
ter responsible. On the other hand, it seemed extremely unlikely
that such a message had been programmed into it.

Goss was standing by the window puzzling over the notice,
when he saw the meter man crossing the yard in the opposite
direction. Goss remembered he had seen him a moment before
striding across the yard, already with his book out. He must have
made the entry very quickly. Seeing him hurry by, Goss went to
the door, intending to question him about the sheet of paper, and
actually holding it up and flourishing it as he rushed out. But
already the pickup truck was moving down the road.

2

Several months passed. There were no more out-of-the-way
bills. This was a relief. On the other hand, things were not totally
as they had been before. Toward the end of each month, the bill
from the utility company would arrive. It was a powder-blue or a
mat-grayish sheet with the titles, etc., printed in deep blue in
boldface, with white areas or columns under the kilowatt hours
and the rate. A perfectly uniform and unvarying sheet except for
the monthly charges typed on it in black ink. There were no
charges for "externalities."

Still, there was the possibility that something of the sort could
have appeared. The first message had been there, positioned one-
third of the way down, starting at the left margin and extending
the width of the page into the white columns. The fact that it did

not appear in subsequent billings was an indication that the first message had been a mistake, though an alarming one. Goss had paid the bill and decided to wait before making inquiries. If there were no more bills, he could put it down to being simply an error. There was no need to worry about it.

On the other hand, he couldn't help but be curious about the information, particularly the figure of $31 for the eight villagers. If it were only an individual bill—his own—that would put the cost of exterminating the villagers at around $4 a person. The figure seemed low. But if it were an averaged figure and the charge spread out over all the customers—there were approximately a hundred thousand customers in the utility company— it was outrageously high. On the other hand, it was possible that the casualty figure itself could have been similarly averaged out, so that the eight villagers listed on the sheet represented only the fraction of the total that was his responsibility and covered his own charge—a possibility he hated to think about.

The information on the first bill had been scanty, so that it was possible that future bills would contain information which might clear up some of these points. Also, he was intrigued by the phrase "ongoing credit account." He hadn't realized he had such an ongoing credit, though this was possible and that it kept balancing itself out in the normal course of things. If it had come to light, it was probably because he had fallen behind in his payment for a month, or his letter had been delayed through being addressed to the wrong zip code. If so, this could have been going on for months or even years. In which case the total amount would be staggering. He probably could have wiped out a whole village.

However, no more bills with messages of this kind came. Goss was pleased with his strategy of waiting, which he felt was justified. If there was a repetition, this would prove that what was purported to have happened was a fact, and he would have to face up to it. If nothing further occurred, it would be a strong indication that it had been simply an event or "anomaly," as Goss liked to call it. It would not be necessary to believe in it.

Several more months passed. Goss was relieved. Then he received his October bill. He ripped it open along with a batch of other mail which he had just gotten, standing by the window overlooking the yard. It contained the information

1-1/2 villager killed. Re-supply $6

along with the identical note as to the deduction from his ongoing credit account.

3

Goss was uncertain what the result was of his showing the meter reader this second bill. Luckily he had seen him (he had already checked the meter) and managed to stop the man in midcourse. The meter man had stared as Goss held it in front of him—or possibly he had taken it in his hand and held it up to the light. Goss could not be sure from his expression whether he understood the position Goss had been put in as regards the "externalities" and whether he sympathized with him. Or whether he was annoyed by being shown the paper. It was not his business. Or he may have been simply indifferent, and had not even read the bill. He handed it back and said only: "Have you called Billing?"—the words delivered while the man was already moving away.

This was to be expected. Goss reflected that in all the years the man had appeared on the property they had rarely spoken. When they did meet it was Goss that proffered the greeting, a hello or remark on the weather—the meter reader responding without a word, merely a nod. Goss remembered only one conversation with him. It had happened accidentally. Goss had contracted to have his woods cut by a logger with a team of horses. The meter man had made reference to them, allowing that he himself had a team of oxen he used for maple sugaring. He gave a brief description of his operation (Goss was surprised to discover it was substantial), concluding, he was already "tapped out," meaning, spouts were driven into the trees, connected by plastic pipe.

It was late March. Snow was on the ground. Goss, who had hung a few buckets on the trees, asked:

"When will it start running? Any day?"

The meter man thought it was already running in some places.

He had stopped, he said, by a farm down the road. The farmhouse was at the bottom of a hillside with a sugar bush—which was also "tapped out." There was a sugaring house nearby where the sap was boiled off. After reading the meter he had walked over. No smoke was coming out of it. There was no one around; the door to the shed was shut. He had stood in the spring snow to listen. There was a faint sound inside, a hollow, insistent drumming, which now and then swelled to a steady, musical pouring of liquid into the cistern, a signal that the flow of sap had begun.

This intimacy shared with Goss—and the glimpse of a life beyond the formal boundaries of the company—had been quite uncharacteristic and had not been repeated.

In Goss's father's day the meter reader had also been the bill collector, strange as it may seem. In those days he would note the reading and at the same time collect the money, writing out the bill—a copy to the owner and the duplicate to the company. Since the rate was fixed (at a few cents per kilowatt of electricity in those days), there was nothing discretionary about it, no room for making mistakes. It was the same as if the billing had been done in the office. Originally it had been a small company. In fact the company had been started by a citizen of the town, who had built a dam and power station down on the river. This was all reasonable and logical. If asked, the meter reader could explain everything.

Goss remembered his father telling him about it. His father had been on friendly terms with and had actually looked forward to the visits of the meter man. In those days he would appear at the door (the meter reading and the presentation of the bill were a single event). Goss pictured the man knocking, his father going out, and the two of them chatting in the yard together. His parents had lived there but there had been a divorce, and after that his father had been in the house alone. At that time there were thick woods; the house was far away from town. His father would have been happy with the visits of the meter reader, to make friends with him. He was probably lonely. He lived in the front room, sleeping there, smoking cigars and cooking on a kerosene stove. Goss could imagine his father inviting the man in to sit down for a bite to eat.

Now the company had grown. Now there was a separate department and separate number for the customers to call about billing. And this—inquiries or questions about bills—had become routine. The functions were separate. The meter was read by one person, bills were made out by another, and repairs and maintenance were the responsibility of another department.

Goss had some experience in dealing with the repairs department. Once a line had been down and he had phoned the number listed in the telephone directory for emergency repairs. He explained that a tree had fallen on the line during a storm. The maintenance crew came right away. It was during the night, with the snow still falling. His wife was away. Goss was waiting in his house in the dark lamenting his bad luck. (The power failure had occurred while he was using his electric typewriter.) Down the road he could hear the sound of their truck as it pulled up by the woods and he could see the glow of headlights through the trees. He had gone down to watch them briefly: in the bitter cold one man holding a rope, breath steaming in the headlights; and another leaning backwards from the top of the pole. Then he had returned to the house and remained in the dark for what seemed an interminable length of time. He had expected them to check in with him, tell him the line was repaired and they would make the connection at the transformer by the highway. He was looking forward to thanking them and offering them a hot drink or a shot of whiskey as a comradely gesture. Goss was sitting in the dark staring at the glimmer of a single candle. Suddenly the lights came on, as if by magic. They had simply completed the job and driven off.

He felt cheated. He himself had come out in the cold, stood at the edge of the clearing to make a kind of contact with them. Why should they care about him? He was in full light but with a feeling of loneliness. It was as if in a way this was measured by the slow rotation of the electric meter.

Though he had inherited the electrical system, and the billing procedure had been worked out for a period of years, occasionally something went wrong. Goss was not hesitant about calling the utility company's office in the nearby town of Bradford. In fact he enjoyed it. Usually it was about some trivial matter, an error in the bill that could easily be cleared up by one of the clerks. There was a young woman in the office he generally spoke with—her name was Martha. He knew her voice. She was easy to deal with, sympathetic. He looked forward to some discrepancy he had discovered in checking the figures on his home computer. (Goss fancied himself something of a mathematician.) He would call to Martha's attention some obvious error, with glee. Of course these were routine questions. No doubt there were more difficult ones which were outside the guidelines of the lower-level personnel to deal with. He had called Billing not long ago about what he thought was an overcharge. He had hoped to talk to Martha. She had been out to lunch, and he had spoken with another young woman—who before he knew it had referred him to her supervisor. A Miss Johnson. This conversation had been a disaster. Goss was convinced he was in the right. The record was clear. He had checked all his figures, which he had right in front of him. Goss laid out for her his case. For the period beginning in December the amount of the bill had gone up sharply, though he had used less electricity. (It was while his family was away visiting relatives in Florida.) There must be an error somewhere.

Goss ended triumphantly: "The amount of my bill has doubled when my consumption of kilowatts has gone down!" It was explained by the official that this was due to a seasonal adjustment in rates, which had been higher during the winter months. There was the appearance that he was overcharged when actually the charges were normal, even generous. This was because it was a period of cold when there was the maximum use of appliances.

"But I don't space heat with electricity," Goss protested with an edge of superiority to his voice. "My personal consumption in the winter . . . "

"What you consume personally doesn't matter. The utility company goes by the law of averages. Your experience of the winter is not the statistical experience."

Goss was outraged. He resolved never to ask a question of the company again—at least above the level of Martha. He visualized the office of the supervisor—that is, Miss Johnson—as a kind of dark maze or trap in which the perplexed customer was bound to get further lost.

Still, Goss told himself, this was what he should have expected.

The supervisor had conducted herself reasonably. Martha's role (given her inferior set of guidelines) was to be accommodating, even admiring and flattering should the occasion arise. But when it came to the larger issues of customer relations, other methods came into play. There was a different set of guidelines. Goss had been wrong. But even if she had not known the answer, Miss Johnson would have explained the matter to him in some irrefutable manner. It was impossible to win at this level of company policy. Even if it had not been company policy, simply a cosmic error, she would have concealed it from him anyway. The purpose of the supervisor was to obstruct the flow of information as well as to expedite it.

4

One day Goss and his wife were returning from the weekly trip to the supermarket. He disliked this event. The size of the building depressed him. It meant contending with crowds of shoppers, the traffic in the parking lot. As they came up their driveway through the wood around the curve, Goss was looking ahead toward the house and parking area. He thought he might see the service company's truck.

"He's not here again today. The meter reader. If he were here we'd probably miss him. He's distinguished by his quality of absence."

Goss told his wife the sugaring story, where, with the family gone, the man had stood outside the closed sugar house in the spring snow and listened to the running of the sap.

"You have the feeling that he observes everything, but from a distance. He's not there to communicate—if he's there at all."

"He's not supposed to communicate," Goss's wife told him.

"I would have liked to have discussed it, the externalities, with him at greater length, ask him what he felt about it. But all he did was refer me to Billing. It's obvious you're not going to get to the heart of the mystery there."

"The more you worry the less you solve," his wife suggested.

"Well, it was such a small amount on the two bills—the figures charged for each villager—though even the figures are open to

question. Such a modest amount to be billed, and so many poten-
tial hassles . . . it was probably sound policy to pay and not ask
questions."

"*I'd* have asked questions," Goss's wife told him.

"The bill is for us all."

Goss remembered when he had shown the meter man his se-
cond bill. He was not sure then what his reaction had been. He
may not have cared. But he may have been startled and even
frightened. Was the meter reader trying to avoid him? This was
possible given the man's extremely reticent character. Goss had
brought the man in on his personal financial troubles and what-
ever private agony he might be suffering because of the casual-
ties in *Jinoteca*. That was beyond the bounds of the formal
relationship of service personnel and customer, and certainly
constituted a breach of taste. The meter reader may have taken
Goss's outburst as an infringement of those limits. He may have
thought of Goss himself as an anomaly.

Goss doubted this. A simpler explanation for the employee's
reaction was irritation. Along the route there were many meters
to read. With many new houses built, there probably was a job
speed-up. Then too Goss had been one of the earliest hook-ups
for the electric company when the customers were mostly farms.
Goss's pole was far from the highway through the woods. The
line had been knocked down several times in storms, so they lost
money. So as far as the utility company was concerned, as a
customer Goss was marginal. Possibly they had even told the
meter reader not to talk to Goss.

Still, the bills continued to nag him. There had been no more
out-of-the-way bills. The monthly blue-grey statements from the
electrical company were normal: blank and empty except for the
print-out of kilowatt hours and charges. Now the blankness and
emptiness was a factor that worried Goss. If the casualties were
not listed on the ordinary bill, might they not be there just the
same—but latent—on the "ongoing credit account" continuously
being balanced and cancelled out? Wasn't it a possibility at least
that the blank and unoffending bill was a continuous record of
casualties? So with the benefit of the light came this profound
mystery and deeper puzzle. Still, the surprising thing was that

the "externalities" had appeared in the bill in the first place. This had been the untoward event: that it had come to light. And Goss would have preferred that it had remained hidden.

It's true that Goss, if he had run into the meter man, might have asked him about his ongoing account and whether it had been there in his father's day. But it was not the same meter man.

Was there some reason for the meter reader's disappearance? It occurred to Goss he may have been let go. The fact that the meter man had come might be deduced from the fact that there was a bill, that the kilowatt hours this month were different from the preceding month. But this could have been recorded mechanically. With advances in technology it was conceivable that Goss's meter could have been monitored from somewhere else, from the office in Bradford, and billed directly. That would make sense as far as cost efficiency was concerned. So there would be no need for field work and the meter man's function would be superfluous. This was technically possible. He would stop coming; the customer would never be the wiser. Still, there would be some resistance on the part of the customer: the human witness as a guarantee against mechanical failure. And because—as in Goss's case—the customer had become attached to him. So the meter reader would have been retained for purely sentimental reasons.

5

His family had given Goss a pair of binoculars for his birthday. German made. Prismatic lens, with a 7x35 magnification. They were for watching birds. Goss often stood by the window, the top half pulled down, when he heard bird song. Resting his elbows on the wooden sash, he would cruise the nearby woods searching for the wren or song sparrow. To the center there was a more distant view over the fields—tops of elm trees and hills, continuous shifts of color.

Seeing him stationed at the window, his wife asked him how he liked the binoculars.

Goss told her, "Superb. Now I'm able to see things, locate them, and catch them in the lens exactly. Before there was only this mysterious sound—mysterious in the sense I didn't know where it was coming from. Now I can identify what bird is singing and even watch the notes pour out of its throat."

His eldest daughter had been to a restaurant the evening before where they played music. It was called Waterworks. The daughter followed the local bands. The one performing currently was the Rude Girls, who were beginning to make a name for themselves.

"It was packed. We had to stand by the bar. But it was terrific." The daughter said she thought she had seen Miss Johnson.

Goss expressed surprise. "That's the last person I'd expect to be there."

"Why? Or why not? It was advertised both in the paper and on the radio, the date of the concert. There was a picture of the Rude Girls plastered on store windows."

"I suppose anybody could have seen them," Goss acknowledged. "And if they liked that sort of thing . . . "

"She was with a date."

"What kind of date?"

Goss's daughter worked as a waitress. "I've seen him around. He's kind of a smoothy and man-about-town. A heart-breaker, I'd say."

"At a concert?" (Goss had never seen Miss Johnson.) "She must take time out from the office. I wouldn't have thought. . . . Well, I might have guessed she needed entertainment . . . some companion she went out with. Though she has a forbidding personality. Probably the call to music was overwhelming."

"They go there a lot. She and the guy must be in the inner circle, know the performers. During the intermission one of the Rude Girls was sitting at their table. I couldn't tell if they were talking. They have a little dance floor at the far end; people danced."

Again Goss said, "I'm amazed."

"After the concert began again we got a seat. As we squeezed through we passed them. She had her handkerchief to her eyes. She was crying—had turned her face away from the Rude Girls, from the spotlight. Her mascara was running."

There was a pile of bills on the table. All at once there was a bird trilling in the trees. Goss picked up his binoculars.

"What kind of bird?"

"I can't tell. From the markings I'd say a red poll or a siskin. From the cry it could be a song sparrow. If only it would hold still."

In front of the house the ground fell away. So the binoculars' line of sight was directly into a wall of branches. Goss oriented himself by the distant hill, then swept backward and to the right again. Immediately he was traveling through the woods, a maze of impenetrable leaves, darks and lights, foreground and depths— trying to sight the elusive bird.

Suddenly a shape intervened. The picture blurred as if a wad of cotton were drawn across the lens. Swiveling, Goss tracked it— at the same time bringing his binoculars into focus and following the figure as it moved across the yard. It was the meter reader.

The meter man comes into focus. He is on the way to read the meter on his monthly rounds. Utility pole behind in the grass. The owner will go out into the yard, greet him. The two of them will stand as the meter is read.

As if Goss, the customer of electricity, is pulled into the event, the occasion, by the current itself. And the meter reader, in his mid-afternoon rounds, has been pulled out of the pickup truck, out of his own reveries, into the same force field. The flow toward the meter which began afar off and in mysterious processes . . . the uranium mines, oil refineries, or the tons of hurtling-down white Canadian water power, propelled by the same destiny.

Man in early thirties, square face, somewhat guarded look, compact build. Moves with the arms swinging, neck and weight forward. Straight line shortest distance. Job to be done. Now has been trapped by Goss; he can't escape. Nor for three minutes regain the refuge of the truck. He walks with a limp, an awkward plunging movement, which to Goss seems graceful or mythical. Heavy black lumberjack boots waterproofed with mink oil. Checkered green and blue shirt. Red suspenders. Baseball cap.

His goal the pole out back. Seriously weathered over the decades, may need a replacement. Overhead cables stretching to infinity, lines across the sky, perch of small birds.

Plunging over the grass, covers the space from the company

vehicle to utility pole and back. What we'd call "reading the meter" consisting of standing before the instrument with feet planted, focusing of the eyes, noting down the number of kilowatt hours in decimals: tens, hundreds, thousands, corresponding to days, hours and minutes, and jotting them down on the lined notebook which he has flipped out and holds in front of him. Pages identified with numbers and names of customers along the route. This page marked GOSS.

TESTIMONIO

As I Lay Dying

> Jinoteca
> Nicaragua
> 9/3/87 thru 10/3/87

Billed to H. Goss

As I lay dying. The pain. That, first of all. The sky beyond the trees. The trees merged with the roofs of houses which were of a blue color. I can describe, also, the earth on which I was lying. The earth was the main thing. It was a dried, stiff mud which was holding me up. It had a grip like a strong man's or like the jaws of an animal, a bullock or a horse. I was gripped by it. But it didn't want to bite me. On the contrary, it loved me. It wanted to help me.

The earth was discolored by a trickle of my blood which threaded into a pool in the dust almost at a level with my eyes. It was just lying there filling. It was as if it didn't come out of me, it had no connection with my life. The pain was in one place and the earth and I were in another. But I kept calling

ANTONIA! ANTONIA!

I expected she would come out the door. But I could also see her running through a thicket beyond the coffee plantation ducking through the dense undergrowth with the kids. The kids all getting lost and falling into hiding places, like *garrobos* and chickens, so the soldiers couldn't find them. That gave me pleasure.

The town was absolutely still. Not even the dead moved. Everything was tranquil.

The pool was powdered with a film of brownish-red dust. This could have been in my own eyes. Because they were bleeding. Or maybe they just wanted to bleed, because they wanted to grieve.

Partly because it reflected the sorrow of my hand—which lay a little further off on the stiff earth, toward home. Its fingers were stretched out as if they were asking for a slice of bread.

I no longer expected anyone to come. The town was cleaned out. But I kept raising my arm, waving it around like it was a flag that would attract rescue, and hollering. My eye also saw this blue sky which was collapsing very fast and filling up my house. Came rushing over me with the sound of gunfire.

Into the pool drop by drop.

THE METER

round molded glass   light along the curve silver or mercury gleam   sticking out 5 inches from the box   glass cylinder transparency perfect rondure   A big eye with its ultramarine depths   darknesses   Inside:
THE ACTIVE THING
Transparent glass against neutral gray metal box enamel tint   the word MILBANK   stamped lower lefthand corner identifies the manufacturer   Box mounted onto the side of the house or pole   with the cable penetrating descending entering leaving   Plastic sheath   also subdued shiny gloss equally gray the one cable goes off everywhere to distant points beyond eye focus   the other looping into the house

All quiet subdued neutral inert   Except the active element
        the disc rotating inside
cast metal mouth   pinched at the center   Here black vertical stroke to mark or tick off
    a single rotation as it spins by
            counter clockwise
perforated disc flat spin seen on edge little nebula

    in an interior black sky
In the immobility of the object   *this*
          is the only thing that moves
    And behind   darkness
sea cave with its lights and shadows
    where the invisible and hidden is measured

Glass container centered below rhomboid plate
bearing the company name and legend
    SANGAMO
single phase   15 amperes
watt hour meter   240 volts 3-wire
type 1-30-3   model AR5
                  (some small words not decipherable)
    23 081 739
    below this crudely stamped number
    44 746
At the top of the glass shield with four circles printed on it
    clockface   each identical   0 through 9   but with hands
pointing at different numerals

left   left   right   right
bottom 4   top 7.5   top 6   bottom 6.6

single black hand nailed to center of each circle

    four clocks touching forming an arc or crescent
        to frame the words
        KILOWATT HOURS
At bottom of box little latch   plastic seal

■ The Hostage

Will and Judith Sommers were making breakfast in the kitchen. It was already light and the tree at the edge of the road stood out.

"Should we wake him?"

"I think he's already up." The ear of the mother was the more acute. The child was sitting at the edge of the bed putting on his slippers.

It was since he had started school that the child had been given his own room, which was always cluttered. He was an avid reader of books and liked to read at night. In this, he had already acquired adult habits.

The father was fully dressed and even had his cap on. He had been out to the woodshed and started the fire in the stove. Judith Sommers stood beside the tea kettle, not yet awake, her bathrobe held around her with one hand. There were now distinct sounds from the boy's room.

So far they had been speaking in whispers in the dimly lit kitchen—though the object of everything was to get the child up and moving. It was not often that the father—worried he might not make it in time—would go into the room himself and wake the boy, stroking his head, gently shaking him and watching until the small bundle under the covers stirred. The parents' whispers were partly from habit, and partly that on this particular morning there were guests in the bedroom upstairs. They had been up late the night before. When the other couple had gone to bed, Judith had called up to them, "Sleep as late as you want. After all, you don't have to make the school bus. You can have breakfast whenever you come down."

The other couple had known the Sommerses many years before in Wisconsin.

The seacoast town was at the far end of a peninsula, and though it could be reached by car, the trip across the water by ferry was easier. The boat had docked. And when the visitors had stepped ashore, they had been surprised to see the Sommerses with a small boy holding the father's and the mother's hands, his chin pressed against the railing. Will Sommers was considerably older than his wife, had been married before and had not wanted to have a child.

When they had gone up to their room, getting ready for bed, the two had talked about this. The woman recalled what Judith had confided to her. And added, "He was quite positive about it. Judith told me. Of course she was sad about it."

The man said, "Well, now it seems he's quite happy with the child."

The day before, the Wisconsin couple had been shown what the Sommerses called "the homestead." This consisted of a serious vegetable garden, an apple orchard, and a hay field, on which were tethered a few goats. The Sommerses tried to be as self-sufficient in food as possible. Will Sommers did the repair work and upkeep of the house. They required very little in the way of consumer goods. Even clothes were hand-me-downs from neighbors.

All this was done in order to live on the minimum income— as Judith explained—below which they would not be required to pay taxes. So much of the taxes were related to war and to violence directed against people in other countries. None of this took their visitors by surprise. When they had known the Sommerses before in Wisconsin, they had been involved in antiwar protests and had been interested in tax refusal. They remembered them both as being spirited people willing to act on their beliefs, and therefore somewhat exceptional.

The Sommerses had tried a number of ways, but none of the half-measures worked. The government always got its money. And the money in one way or another went towards war. Everyone participated, as they earned money and paid taxes. So they had simply cut out from the system altogether. Will had given up his small business. She had reduced her three days a week book-keeper's job at the pharmacy to one. She had persuaded her employer that she could still do the same amount of work and be paid less.

"Of course, he was delighted. We seem to be the only people in town trying not to make money," Judith said with a laugh.

They were in the vegetable garden picking beans, the two old friends helping as they listened to her. Will, in the same battered hat, was on his knees pulling out weeds. He seemed to them even more gaunt and taller than they remembered him. Clearly the Sommerses were in accord as to what they had made of their life. They had no regrets. Since to live within the system was to contribute to the world's evil, they had opted out of the system. The decision to lead a life of voluntary poverty seemed only practical.

"We don't pretend it's easy. It's hard work. But not that different from life in the old days. Then life was harder, but the moral choices were easier. The world was not so complex. And you know," Judith went on, "as far as this place is concerned—and living off the farm, or from the sea for that matter—well, all the households in town did that a hundred years ago. We've just put the clock back. I'll tell you, it gives us a great sense of relief to be out of it."

"Still, it must cut you off from other people? From the town?" her friend asked.

"Will feels it more. He was very good at what he did. He had a computer business in town and now he grafts apples. No. We don't judge them. What anyone else does is their own business."

"What *is* the IRS minimum?" the man asked.

"Thirty-eight hundred dollars."

The garden was on a slight rise. From where they were standing they could see the sea, the road running along the beach, and the first houses of the seacoast town. The harbor was shrouded in fog.

"On this part of the Maine seacoast," Judith told them, "we have extraordinary tides."

When the Sommerses had arrived five years ago, it was foggy, and they had been guided into the harbor by the tolling of a bell.

The tolling of the bell was restful. This feeling came also no doubt from the reduced speed with which the boat approached the dock, its motion one of slowly gliding. Will had been sitting by the rail reading a newspaper account of the Bhopal Indian chemical plant disaster. The sheer magnitude in numbers was incomprehensible. Two things struck him in particular; that since the chemical—used to manufacture insecticides—produced a heavy discharge from the eyes and accumulated fluid in the lungs, these were technically deaths by drowning. And that the streets of the city, the poorer sections near the plant, were littered with corpses, not only of humans, but of chickens, dogs, cats, cows, and water buffalo killed by the gas.

All of them had been sleeping. The cloud had simply materialized during their sleep. He wondered how they would be disposed of.

Sommers had meant to show the newspaper to his wife. She had gone up to the front. He was leaning against the rail of the ship's stern. Somehow or other the newspaper slipped off and dropped into the water, as they maneuvered into the dock. It was buoyed up, floated for a moment, then submerged. He watched the headlines gradually disappear in the water.

He had bought the paper in the city on the mainland. When they landed, the small seacoast town looked like a place where they might not sell newspapers. But the tragedy had occupied the media for a number of days.

"Eat up, Zeke. You'll miss the bus."

The little boy was not disposed to hurry. His father sat beside the boy at the table, one of his large hands next to the dish of untouched oatmeal, as if this gesture would encourage the boy to eat.

"You like it with brown sugar. Do you want the milk warmed?"

"You can't push him, Will," Judith Sommers said with some annoyance. But she also would have liked to see the child hurry. She had gone into his bedroom and collected whatever extra clothes he would need and the bag for the school bus. Zeke had certain favorite puzzles and pencils. These it was imperative he take along with him.

"Do you have your sweater? You don't want to go to school on an empty stomach?" the father urged.

Uninterested in the food and unconcerned apparently with the discussion going on around him, the boy sat with his chin almost in the plate and his eyes on one of the illustrations in the storybook, which completely occupied his attention. He was content to be nourished from images.

He was in another world, not at the table.

The parents had long noted this tendency in the child to be absorbed. It gave him a preoccupied or precocious air, and was the source of some trouble at school. In the playground he had been bullied by some of the older boys and the parents had gone to the principal to complain. They had not heard about the trouble from Zeke but from another parent. As for his treatment at the hands of the other school children, Zeke was a philosopher.

He had weak arches, which afflicted him more at some times than others. On the first day he had arrived in the school yard carried in his father's arms. Perhaps this had been the source of the difficulties.

The family downstairs spoke in low tones because of the upstairs guests.

The boy had made some progress with his cereal, taking a few bites. He had pushed the brown sugar into some sort of pattern he was contemplating. Suddenly, puffing out his cheeks and raising his eyes, he gave his mother a big grin.

"Come, Zeke. Don't clown." The mother was sterner with the child than the father was. She was onto his tricks. She considered that Will spoiled Zeke.

Now his father was kneeling, tying his shoes. Zeke, his eyes still on his mother as if they were sharing some secret joke, allowed himself to be pulled and pushed into his jacket. This daily routine occupied all equally. It was a scene where the small boy was the central object, and in which both parents wavered between love and exasperation.

"There goes the bus. Hurry!"

The mother stood in the open doorway, pulling her bathrobe around her throat. In the old days, the father would have left for work after putting the boy on the school bus.

She watched them through the window as they went down toward the road. Her eye followed the two figures, which were simply one figure, the child bundled up and securely buttoned, the man thin and without a jacket, and probably cold. The father stooped over the son and held him by the hand.

The Sommerses house was the last one on the route, and Zeke was the last student on the road to be picked up. The bus went by the house and went a little further up the road, where it would turn around and then come back.

Each day the two waited for the bus. They could hear it through the trees. Then rattling around the curve, it appeared. In another moment it had stopped, the hood of the engine shaking. The dirty yellow surface before them was like a wall blocking everything else from view. High up in this wall the windows, and a row of children's faces looking out at them. The children's curiosity contrasted with the indifference of the driver, who sat with his hands in his lap looking at the road. The two would stand there for a moment across from it, submitting to inspection by the bus passengers, or as if immobilized by the sheer size of the bus, yellow against the green shoreline and trees muted by the early morning fog. The scene was repeated at the same time each day, like clockwork.

Then the little boy scurried in front, lugging his satchel, and was momentarily lost to view. To the father it was as if the new passenger was being swallowed up and digested in the dark interior. He had lost him. Then after a moment, a small face appeared in the window. It was Zeke. He gazed solemnly down. From behind the glass, he gave his father an absorbed look which lasted while the bus pulled away and the father continued to stand there, his hand raised. Will Sommers watched the bus slowly draw away from him down the road along the seashore.

The little boy looked at them through the window of the school bus as if they were a picture from some storybook. Or the remains of some vast shipwreck the waves had cast ashore. The road ran along the breakwater and below that was the beach. Along the high water mark, the bodies lay in a ragged line like the seaweed left at high tide, some of them touching the embankment.

The great stretch of beach lay exposed at the ebb tide. This also was covered with scattered bodies. The sea had retreated leaving the empty beach. Almost level, with its barely descending slope, it simply extended outward into the fog. There was no ending to the sand. No horizon line. There was simply the beach disappearing into the dense bank of fog.

The townspeople were already down on the beach, either curious or indifferent, examining the bodies. They walked around them. Some had even begun to cart them away. It was impossible to tell—from the gravity and concentration of the children's faces looking out the window—whether this was extraordinary, or was a scene they saw every day. Or whether for the people of the seacoast town, who were probably accustomed to shipwrecks, this was a familiar task. The bodies had been left by the sea. But the sea had already retreated behind the dense bank of slightly yellowish fog.

There were also lobster pots on the beach. And some fishermen's dories tilted on their sides, tethered to an anchor by a long rope—which the tide would float when it returned. Some of the bodies lay face down in the shallow tidal pools, or blocking the grey ribs of sand where rivulets of salt water still drained or fanned out with the ebb tide. They were mostly children and old people, some naked, some clothed in their dhotis. The living seagulls strutted among the dead. There were also other birds and animals. A bullock lay on its side, its legs stiff.

Some of the seagulls perched on the bodies or from the sand picked at the hand of a castaway that lay empty. The detachment of the gulls seemed to relate somehow to the detachment of the townspeople. Or perhaps the low grey cloud or fog bank framed them in a single picture.

The dead littered the sand floor as far as the eye could see. There was no line between the sand and the sea. There was no sky or sea, only the fog which had drifted in during the night. It was as if the bodies were not the gift of a shipwreck or from some distant storm. They had simply materialized. They had been dumped there. They had simply been unrolled from the base of the poison cloud.

■ Guatemala

Evelyn had been to a shop named TRAJE which sold native Central American clothes and handcrafts. It was owned by a friend who had recently returned from Guatemala, from a buying trip to the highlands area northwest of the capital, where there were Indian villages. On the wall of the shop were stunning black and white photographs of Quiché Mayan women in their native robes and headdresses consisting of strands of woven cloth twisted in knots.

Evelyn stood admiring the photographs. "You were in that part of the country? I would have thought it was dangerous with a camera."

The shop owner, Hammer, had been going on his buying trips once or twice a year for the past several years. He knew the score perfectly. Among the photos there were one or two scenes of villages showing an angled street with its cobbles and rows of adobe houses. There were few people in the street.

Evelyn had heard enough about what was going on in the country and the activities of the soldiers, to be surprised.

"I should think," Evelyn went on, "that the last thing you'd want to be doing with the National Guard around is taking photographs."

Hammer grinned. One of the photos was taken from the rear of a group of guardsmen, a close-up of the backs of their necks and their wide belts and pistol holders. The photographer also looked at the photograph.

"If you act like a tourist you can do anything. Travelers don't get up in the hills that often, but when they come to a picturesque village, you can bet they have their cameras out and clicking away a mile a minute. The soldiers are even pleased. They take it as a sign of innocence."

"But that doesn't go so far as speaking to a villager," Evelyn objected. "How would a tourist speak with them? But these individual portraits . . . "

Hammer was not the only buyer of native crafts who came there from North America. Since he had traveled to many of the villages before the massacres—which began in 1978 under Rios Montt—he continued to go there. And that was true of a number of the buyers. But things were not as they were. Whole villages had disappeared. Nevertheless, even though the *mercado* in the village may not have had as much to offer as before, there were still peasant women who wove cloth and had their weaving to sell.

There was also the factor of business and the income to the government from the export of handcrafts. The authorities had a good deal of respect for and understanding of businessmen from North America, and occasionally an adventurous one would be found in a remote Mayan village.

In the store, TRAJE, the portraits of native women were handsome in their *cortes* and *huipils*, handwoven with the traditional pattern of each village. An elegance. The pictures were posed in such a way and with such skill that it gave the onlooker a sensation of tranquility and even joy.

A woman of Evelyn's acquaintance had been on the trip to Nicaragua and had written an account in the local paper. There were a number of organizations opposing United States intervention in the region. Often these were connected to Latin American women's organizations, such as "Madres de la Plaza del Mayo" in Argentina, and in Chile, "Familiares de los Desparecidos," women family members of those who had "disappeared."

As the North American women's group was not allowed to go to the country directly by air, they had first flown to El Salvador. There they had made a tour of a women's prison.

While we were there we visited the women's prison of Illopango. After the streets of San Salvador, where every street corner is

guarded by soldiers and patrolled by police vehicles, the atmos-
phere inside the prison seemed positively free. It appeared to be
run by the prisoners themselves, members of the FMLN—the
Frente Farabundo Marti de Liberacion National—but this was the
result of a hunger strike that had just occurred.

Most of the women had lost husbands or children, or had been
wounded in the war themselves. We were particularly struck by
a young woman with one leg, in a colored print dress. She had
been raped and then shot. She was with her mother, who fussed
over her—she was young and very shy—and encouraged her to
recount her experience. There were several legless women there
who took turns using the single pair of crutches. The atmosphere
was generally lively and friendly, with many children running
around. We heard an older woman call them "children of shame;"
that is, of rape by soldiers. But this was vehemently disputed by
a young black-tammed woman who was a commandante, cap-
tured in the mountains. "We are all of us children of shame in El
Salvador."

But the traveler who had written this account remembered it
somewhat differently when telling it to friends. There was a
different slant to it. She had been impressed by the outrageous
and humorous behavior of this "little commandante" who lorded
over the other prisoners and encouraged them to tell their stories
to the North Americans. A chorus had even sung the anthem of
the Farabundo Marti Front. The atmosphere, as often in such
international meetings of groups of women, was one of liveliness
and comraderie. It was more like a common room or a nursery
with children running around.

An amusing incident occurred. In the room was a big TV
screen. None of the poor women would have owned a TV. They
were mostly peasants. But there were a few with a fairly sophis-
ticated knowledge of the U.S. One of the members of the visiting
North Americans was a TV actress who had appeared in a serial.
During the interview there had been whispers among the prison-
ers. The woman had been pointed to. "Don't we know her? Hey,
haven't we seen her someplace?"

The stories of the atrocities continued. Finally one of them
yelled: "Hey! It was on TV!" They named some show, at which

point the actress was recognized by all of them. She was flattered and pleased. And there was much yelling and laughter.

The store, TRAJE, might have attracted someone going by casually in the street with its display window and glimpse behind this of a packed multicolored chamber where everything offered itself but nothing was known. Everything was unfamiliar, yet everything, in one way or another, came from the world of everyday where clothes were worn and, with a gesture a scarf was thrown over a person's shoulder.

Generally Hammer's store was not a place for strangers or tourists. It served a settled population in the region. Often a customer who came in was someone Hammer knew, either socially or from some march or political demonstration. As often as not they would come to talk as much as to buy something.

From his place at the counter Hammer was watching a couple, a man and his wife, apparently attracted by the photographs. They stood looking at them. Then the woman (they were an older couple) moved off, to browse through the store.

The space was small and so crammed full of merchandise it was more like a storeroom or cabin in a ship. There were also racks of dresses up to the ceiling. On shelves were woolen sweaters, scarves (Mexican *raboso*) the color of lemons, limes, and plums. There were Peruvian domed caps and knitted leggings. And in a narrow alcove were piles of folded bolts of cloth. These were *cortes*, each woven according to traditional design, and worn by women as skirts. With the *huipil*, blouse, and *cinta* headband, this makes up the whole *traje*, the peasant women's traditional dress.

The man stood in front of the counter and Hammer behind it. The glass case was also full of handcrafts: silver jewelry, small pottery, pitchers whose spouts and handles were animals' heads and tails, gaily painted plaster plaques for Christmas decorations made with tiny figures and bells.

Outside in the empty street the snow had changed to a slanting pattern of sleet.

The woman, who was interested in a wall hanging, had been

going through the piles of woven cloth to find one that was suitable, with Hammer occasionally giving her advice or telling her the price of a cloth.

She was looking over several piles of *cortes*. The folded edges showed different patterns and colors and when she liked one she would pull it out and hold it up, switching it in one way or another to find the right side, and imagining how it would fit the room.

She had found several that were attractive, but had not been able to settle on any one, and continued to search through the pile. She had started at the top of the step ladder and worked her way down. She had noticed and passed by one bolt of cloth, but now she pulled it out and held it up. The color was less bright and the cloth was torn. In this spot it had a different, a thicker texture where it had been mended.

It seemed to her that the garment was flawed, that it had been wounded somehow. It had not occurred to her that the *cortes* were not simply textiles to be sold. They had been worn. The store specialized in handcrafts. It was natural for the customer to assume that the long hours devoted by the peasant women to weaving were to earn money through sale, not to make their own clothes.

Holding it up with the mended part showing, she asked about it, with some sense of dismay. Implying that perhaps there had been a mistake.

Hammer replied coolly and without apology, "Sometimes you run across one like that. You never know. There are times when they want to sell anything."

The tear might have meant something to Hammer—either some vague memory of an exchange in a mountain village, or something more precise, a story that might have been followed further. As if the circumstances of the bolt of cloth were themselves thread woven through some complicated pattern that he might have gone into.

Evelyn had gone with her daughter to an event sponsored by the Quakers. A Guatemalan refugee couple had been staying at a church in the area involved in the sanctuary movement. The couple, who had a small daughter, were to demonstrate the folk arts of dancing and weaving of the Mayan Indians.

The family had been living at the Saint Francis Priory for about a year, and from here they visited other congregations to recount their experiences. It was usually the man who told the story, in a highly charged and dramatized way—perhaps it was some instinct in him of religious fundamentalism or he was like the circuit-riding preachers of former times. The outline of the story was fairly set. But when he came to a certain point—the murder of his brother—his eyes would fill and he would cry.

On this occasion there was no preliminary talk. It was presumed most of the people had heard the refugees. The room behind the regular meeting hall was small, the audience gathered around the edges. The couple, Miguel and Juana, sat in the front row with their child, a little girl with long braids. Pushed up against her mother's knees, she gazed with jet black eyes at the audience as they came in. The woman was reserved. Obviously she was embarrassed. The man appeared quite at home. He would constantly stand, look up smiling into faces and talk with various people he knew.

The room was drab, bare of furniture except chairs. The audience of mostly church people seemed lacking in energy. They had come out of conscientiousness or curiosity, and did not know each other. From the back room two street lamps could be seen dimmed by the heavy snow. The snow was high in the streets.

The Guatemalans' native language was a dialect of *quiché*. They knew the Spanish of the countryside (Ladino) and had picked up some English. They were introduced by the translator—a young college woman—who gave some background information. The couple had been in the U.S. under the protection of their sponsor for about a year. So far they had been fortunate to be left alone by the U.S. Immigration Service (the policy was to send back the refugees to their own country). But now—so they had been told—an agent from the service was in the area and the situation was uncertain.

The two were to perform in their native costume. But in fact they had never performed. The husband stood in the middle of the circle of expectant onlookers, holding out his arm and en-couraging his partner to dance. But she would not or could not. Finally she was persuaded. But the dance was perfunctory. It was without animation, in a style that was rather wooden—and in any case did not last long.

During the dance the strap of the woman's slip or bra kept coming down and showing under the short sleeve, and she had had to push it up. This added to her embarrassment.

The woman's reluctance, her awkwardness in the dance had awakened Evelyn's interest and sympathy. Under the circum-stances Evelyn would have felt the same. Juana had the Indian's broad face, wide mouth, eyes set wide apart, shiny black hair—not caught up in the *cinta* but falling down the back. Her chest was broad and the stiff blouse pushed her breasts wide apart. She wore her *corte* and *huipil*. To perform the dance her husband donned a black felt hat and threw over his shoulder a heavy wool poncho, which he had now removed.

The woman had regained her composure and natural gravity. A hand rested lightly between her knees. The other held the daugh-ter, pulling her in close to her. The hands were strong but not coarsened by labor. In fact, the translator had told them, Juana had been a schoolteacher in her village or *finca*.

Now she began to talk on the subject of weaving. The explana-tion was directed to the women and perhaps that put her at her ease. As she talked she regained confidence, and spoke with con-siderable animation and even charm. In the craft there was a high degree of skill but, also, it gave pleasure. All the Mayan women wove clothes for the family and their clothes were passed down to them from other women, mothers and grandmothers. In a sense, for Guatemalans to survive was to carry on the tradition of weaving.

At the start they had asked that no photographs be taken. Miguel explained through the interpreter that this was because they were in native dress. And since the pattern was different for each village and set by custom, to show this pattern would be to indicate the village and to alert the authorities. He could not, he said, speak in his native language, since this too might identify the couple and endanger whoever it was back in the village who had survived.

Evelyn wondered what they must be feeling and thinking. Their situation was almost unthinkable. How strange it was when the pattern of one's clothes and the rhythms of one's village speech would betray them. For them, their clothes and their language meant their own identity, which they had to conceal.

Evelyn had gone to Hammer's shop to buy her daughter a dress. Her daughter had gone away for the holidays.

Hammer was out, and his assistant was minding the store. She was a young woman whose craft was jewelry making. Through the shop window figures could be seen hurrying by in the cold.

Evelyn looked through the racks of clothing. She knew her daughter would be pleased with a gift from TRAJE. Coming from behind the counter, the assistant stood beside her, talking.

Hammer had gone to a convention of arts and crafts importers from Latin America. Among them some progressive groups with ties to the Indians in the highlands had formed a marketing cooperative. They had already put out a catalog.

"What's the group called?" Evelyn asked. Her fingers lightly separated the blouses on their hangers.

"Daughters of Corn," the salesperson told her.

This was also the title of Hammer's exhibit of photographs of Guatemalan peasant women in their native clothes. The photos had not been taken down. Studying them, Evelyn remembered her first impression and her question to Hammer: Hadn't taking the photographs been dangerous? In almost every native household soldiers had burst in, members of the family had been raped and murdered, they had fled from the village into the jungle, the *selva*. This had of course happened after the North American businessman's visit but not long after.

As if following her thought, the salesperson said, "Hammer told me you were at the Quakers? And that Juana and Miguel gave an exhibit on Mayan dancing."

In Evelyn's and Hammer's circle—which included the assistant—the names of the Guatemalan refugee couple would have been known. In fact they were made-up names.

"It wasn't very successful. But, of course, it was touching," Evelyn told her, thinking at the same time how extraordinary it was that the refugees had told their story at all. And perhaps the telling of the story, as in some way a sequential history, was the drama itself—that it could now be spoken of. The massacre of Indians and the destruction of villages had happened so suddenly, on such a large scale, and without apparent reason—that to the victims it must have seemed almost like a natural catastrophe, an earthquake or hurricane.

The young woman was wearing a piece of the store jewelry. It was a necklace with a pendant in the form of a bird. Evelyn remarked on it.

The salesperson said, "Isn't it a fine piece? It's a *quetzal*. Their bird of paradise." The quetzal bird was silver with feathers of brightly colored glass.

The young woman was a friend of Evelyn's daughter. The two of them often went to concerts together. She also worked in silver. Evelyn asked her what she had been doing recently.

The woman complained that, though the jewelry was going well, she didn't have enough time for it. The arts and crafts fairs constantly demanded new lines and she couldn't make enough money at it. Though she liked Hammer and enjoyed being in the store, she would like to have more time to do her own work.

Evelyn knew she had a child to support and that her husband had left her. She was about the same age as her daughter. She was of slight build and had an attractive well-modeled face. Whatever its drawbacks, she seemed to take an interest in the store and to admire what was on display.

With Evelyn the assistant went through the racks of cheerfully patterned blouses, both looking for something they liked. Evelyn had already picked out a skirt.

"Here's one." She held it up.

"Just right for her."

"You don't think it's too bright? You both have the same color hair. Your hair has a little henna in it. I don't know if it's the right size. Are they all the same size?"

"No, I don't think so. I'll try it on and you can see."

Glancing to the side at the mirror, she tried on the *huipil*. And then she also wrapped the *corte* around her to make sure it was not too short, and to give the entire effect of the dress.

"It's not too short?"

"What do you think?" She raised her arms.

Both women looked from the mirror's reflected image to the person modeling the dress.

Standing off, Evelyn could see her daughter in the assistant.

GUATEMALA

42,000 square miles, from ocean to ocean. Port city (on the Atlantic) Puerto Barrios.

Highest point: mountain of Tajumulco on the Pacific cordillera.

Other Indian names (of provinces): Chimaltenango, Quezaltenango, Suchitepéquez, Totonicapán.

And the names of villages: Chtuj, Pol, Xalbal, Chinque, Xacebal, Chitatul, Chujalimil, Chuhueca, Xepocol, Santa Cruz del Quiché, (all of which have disappeared).

Languages: Spanish, Ladino, Quiché

Monetary unit: Quetzal (meaning also bird of paradise or plumed bird). Golden crest. Top feathers green, green of jungles or *selva*. Below, red, as if it had stepped lightly into a river of blood. Plumed tail feathers are carmine, emerald, lemon, black, azure.

Crops of Guatemala: On the seacoast—sugar, cotton. In the highlands—coffee, beans, and corn. Corn used to make liquor, bedding, tortillas. Hung from the roof to dry over the winter.

The corn out of the earth, the Indian women from the same earth.

Names of villages: Chicehl, Caxixay, Santa Tomas Ixcan, Santa Maria Tzeju.

All of them have disappeared.

When he'd gone, her husband had left the ceiling light on. She heard a door slam, the sound of cars in the street. It was broad daylight outside. The shutters were closed. The barred shadow fell over the sheet and over her body.

Evelyn lay on the bed after making love, her legs luxuriously spread, and yawning. She thought of the Guatemalan woman, Juana, making love.

When she got up and went over to the bureau to comb her hair—drawing her hair up at the back in an unconscious gesture, her eyes half-closed, leaning forward into the mirror—she saw another woman standing there. She herself had disappeared.

Over the shoulder of the other woman, slightly above her, hung a clustered object on which the light gleamed. It was ears of corn stripped and tied by their husks, suspended from the ceiling by a cord. It was dark in the room—everything else was in shadow—but somehow there was a gleam on the bare hard kernels. From a post behind her, Evelyn could make out a weaving frame. It stretched out in the darkness. There was a pitcher. There must have been a stove or fireplace; the wall behind was blackened by smoke. In the wall there was a small window showing a patch of sky.

The sky of Guatemala.

The woman looking out at her was not Juana. It was one of the women Evelyn had seen in Hammer's photographs.

The peasant woman was not wearing her traditional *traje*. Her hair was pulled up under a white cotton cloth and her dress was made of sacks of cotton sewn together. There was a tear in the cloth. Evelyn noticed that on the knuckle of one finger there was a lump or growth.

It was not so much of a shock, that she had appeared. But that Evelyn herself had vanished. In the place of her room was this other person's room, with its magical objects: the hanging bundle of corn, the weaving frame, the stove, the pitcher . . .

These were the objects of every day. But they were magical because they were from the everyday life of another person. The sky—which was showing faintly through the window, with its last blue light, or through the cracks in the boards—was the sky of every day. It was the everyday sky of Guatemala.

She was the woman Evelyn had seen in Hammer's photograph. But she had appeared at a time before the photograph was taken, before the soldiers had burst into the room, before there had been a story . . .

There was only the earth of every day, the sky of every day.

The woman was telling Evelyn that she had gotten up that morning before dawn. It was three A.M. The rest of the family was on the dirt floor sleeping. She had ground corn to make tortillas, to eat at home and later in the field, for all of them. In the coffee grove she had worked until two, her baby strapped to her back. Tagging along with her, two of the smaller children. The older ones were picking at another *finca*. She had carried the full coffee sack to the house of the finca owner, and that took two more hours. Then she returned to her house, gathered firewood, and made supper of tortillas and beans, and the family ate it. They were all of them together: the husband, the grandmother, and all the children.

She had labored the whole day, she had gone the whole day without rest, without once resting.

But this was a day, when she looked back on it, that would seem like paradise.

■ Visitors to the Cape

*And the stars that terrify goldfish
are neither for sale nor for lease*
　　　　　　　—Benjamin Peret

LIGHT

　　The young man, a student, said: "I want to go to Mexico. I want to find out who I am." His mother gave him an indulgent smile. She and her friend were preparing a meal in the kitchen alcove off the living room. The young man clasped his knees in his arms, his head thrown back, thinking that finding himself—who he really was—would be a remarkable adventure. But it was one he was already tired of.

　　He was playing a tape of John Coltrane on the stereo.

　　The house had wide glass doors; the upper wall of the living room was also of glass. Through this glowing triangle, the sunlight spilled into the house unblocked by curtains. The clear blue light from the sky. The light, taken up from the nearby sea, was transported and poured into the house in buckets.

　　The family and their guests had been to the bay to dig mussels. The younger mother was suckling her baby. She wore a loose buttonless shirt which was easy to push aside and give the child its dinner without the rigamarole of preparing the meal in the kitchen, blending things and heating them up on the electric stove. She felt completely self-sufficient. The baby's lips on her nipples made a smacking sound. She shifted her weight, at the same time seeing the portrait of herself, her pleasant face and the figure of the nursing baby, reflected in the mirror opposite the window. In the mirror were also reflected the woods and sky.

It was possible the child was older. The family and guests had spent the day at the beach. It was late in the day and the child was cranky. This was the ritual interval before dinner. Rather than a picture of contentment, the child was irritating everybody. She sat on the floor cutting out paper dolls.

The seashore was about a half mile away through the pine woods. The thick forest of pitch pine interspersed with oak and bayberry covered the sandy slopes, running up the hills from the sea. Over this an occasional gull floated or coasted as if blown in from the shore. Sometimes the gull would land on the deck railing.

The student and his sister and her young husband would be gone in a few days. The two guests—an older couple—had just arrived. And in a few days they would also be gone.

"Don't you usually dig for mussels at ebb tide? I had water up to my waist. I had to anchor myself with my feet and explore for the mussels with my toes. And when you bend down the water comes up to your nose."

"Your vegetable garden is doing well. But don't you have a problem with woodchucks?"

"Yes, they come over from the neighbors. For woodchucks, there are no property lines."

"How was the trip down? Did you run into traffic?"

"We were surprised when we got to Truro. How much the town has been built up."

"Yes. Every year it's a shock."

During the summer the guests were continually going in and out. The glass doors that led to the wood deck were continually being opened, then dutifully slid shut. Often there was a wind blowing—the "shore breeze" it was called. This had to be kept out, partly because it was chilly, partly because its force would have invaded the house, filling it suddenly. When this happened it was like a flock of sea birds getting into the room.

The other houses, which were near, could not be seen through the trees. From the wood deck, through a pair of binoculars, a jay or a pileated woodpecker could be observed flitting from tree to tree.

"They have particularly good bluefish at the fish market. It's a specialty."

The mother of the nursing young woman and her friend were preparing dinner in the kitchen alcove off the large room. From time to time, one of them would bring a dish out to the table, glancing briefly at the others. The two women were about the same age. Both had had previous husbands. They talked softly but with intense interest in each other. One of them was plump, laughed a lot, and had a coarse vigor. The other was slim. She walked very gingerly over the brightly polished floor. Due to a childhood injury, she walked with the heel of one foot slightly raised with exaggerated caution as if advancing over ice—at the same time, holding her head and torso very erect. This gave her a somewhat distant and aloof air. In fact, the two women were closest friends, lived near each other in the city. Both had known hard times, near poverty, and some misery with their first husbands, but were now fairly well off and, in the way of the world, quite contented. In fact, these visits, always late in the summer, were arranged for their benefit. So they could see each other and catch up, as if they couldn't bear to be away from each other for more than a few months.

All of the group had been on an excursion to the bay. Or on the ocean side sunbathing and lying on the sand, occasionally going for a dip though it was cold. The two second husbands had strolled together up the beach remarking on the topics of the day and discussing the bathing suits of the sunbathers. Now, however, it was the interval before dinner and they had nothing to say to each other. The nursing mother was preoccupied with herself and the child. The student lay full length on the floor, his eyes closed and his face and ear pressed to the rug (as if—having turned it on—wanting to avoid listening to the music of the black musician). The two men were left alone with each other with nothing to say. They had consented to this visit to the cape out of consideration, out of fondness for their wives. But without the two women as audience and to energize them, they had lost interest. They sat in their chairs on opposite sides of the room. Stiffly. Sealed off from each other. It was as if there were a banner stretched above them, or as if there were, as with figures in the comics, a balloon over their heads which read: "We dislike each other."

Or it was the next morning. The other members of the household were not up yet. The two women had been making breakfast. Now they crossed the living room toward the glass doors. In their nightgowns covered by a bathrobe. In the early morning with the sun barely over the trees. Holding their breakfast trays, they slid the doors open and stepped out on the deck and went over by the railing.

They would sit together talking: about food, shopping at the fish market, and what they would buy; about their grandchildren; about the pleasures and drawbacks of their husbands, and how these related to the children. They sat in the chill air, their bodies protected by terry cloth bathrobes, the coffee cups and saucers on their laps. At the edge of the deck, the wild landscape with its beach plum, its tangle of bayberry and huckleberry, began.

THE PLACE

Now you're out of the house—which is in a way your own skin. You're following a sandy track through the wood—which has been here long before you have. It meanders from house to house, each one hidden from another by the dense grove of pitch pine, briar rose, and thickets of beach plum. This is a city in the woods which has already been deserted. The windows are shuttered. The deck, decorated with lobster buoys, is empty. In the yard there is a fishing boat up on blocks for the winter, or a car covered by worn canvas.

Or, leaving the track, you've cut directly through the woods, followed the jumps of a rabbit or, beckoning among the tree trunks, the red flag of a woodpecker.

The slope is downhill. Arms raised, you're springing over mats of blueberries and huckleberries. And now issuing from the wood into the open, you're another person.

In front of you is the road—which is in a different language.

This is the new road. Asphalt. A dense, uniform black. Its

smoothness not part of the earth but the sky. The road is clean, unmarked by car tracks—like a scrubbed face. The new road, thrown over the shoulder of the hill, is in the language of curves and tangents, of measurements along the center line, of precise gradients. The road is of an absolutely uniform width, with its grass shoulders and lines of underground cables. It is speaking the language of engineering specifications, of property lines drawn by the real estate developer on the map, of codes and engineering permits. (This place will become a new section of the town of Truro.)

But right now it doesn't exist. The plans—which are the reality—have wiped the reality out of existence.

All that is here now is the sand, mats of bayberry and lichens, home of grasshoppers and rabbits. And floating in the blue sky above, a soaring gull. But none of these really exist. They are in the language of nonexistence.

And if you read the signs right you will see houses going up. At intervals along the shoulder of the new road there are enameled metal posts, each one marked OCECO (the Outer Cape Electrical Company). Attached to the power outlet the contractors' equipment; drills, table saws. On the roofs you can hear the carpentry crew of young men banging nails, a racket like a woodpecker.

You can see in your mind's eye a neighborhood at night, lawns, new houses with yellow light emanating from the shades spilling over the shrubs, cars parked under the trees, and kids riding bicycles down the street, maybe peddling toward the bell of a Mr. Softee truck.

At the same time (which is now), the landscape is empty. It is the landscape of blueberries, of the sand hills, the coasting gulls, etc.

You walk along the road and, if you were to meet anybody (he would take your arm and stride along with you), it would be a beefy man with a sanguine complexion and bushy eyebrows. In a salt-and-pepper jacket, crepe-soled boots, smelling of wood smoke. An old settler, a native of the region, now selling real estate. He would spot you for what you are. And gesture up at the sky—which he seems to be offering you, a prospective buyer.

He would take your arm and walk briskly down the road with

you, discoursing on the earth and sky, of the soil and the farmers' bones which lie buried there, the beauty of the landscape and the history of the place from the first settlement.

DARKNESS

We were slipping through the night. It was easy walking over the sand, our feet on a cushion of moss and bayberry. Through the open spaces between trees. We were drifting uphill. The woods had become a core of darkness, each tree holding the darkness in its arms. We moved through it holding up our hands in front of us in case the trees wanted to touch us.

Overhead it was lighter. There were the same stars and sky.

I thought to myself: This is Indian country.

The lighted house was somewhere ahead of us.

The steady breeze from the bay side brought the smell of low water, salt marshes and tidal estuaries, of black mud, of clams.

There's a living to be made there beside the sands.

No matter how you tighten your belt, you're still hungry.

There were other walkers through the trees. If it were daylight, I could see them. If the daylight came and showed everything clearly, we would all be there.

And if it were summer I could reach down through the darkness with my hands and I could pick some blueberries and cram them into my mouth.

Occasionally as we walked I would touch somebody, brush against her bare arm or the fringe of her buckskin sleeve. She was carrying on her shoulder a roll of reed mats that I had seen her weave, which made a tent, a shelter when we moved from place to place. Or maybe there was a baby strapped to her back. In the darkness I could feel its warmth, the pressure of its nose pushed against her back. And that made me wonder: who is she?

There's a tidal pool surrounded by eel grass where you can cast for crabs, crayfish, and small fish. Around it the salt grass stretches away forever, as far as the dunes. Or there are reeds; there is bare clay and an oyster bank.

I ask myself, what is it like to have these copper-colored hands? And I ask myself, what is it like to be balanced at the edge of the pool, your feet splayed, to hurl the net? It circles in the air, drops on the surface of the water, sinks to the bottom closing with its lead weights. And how does it feel to have these hands that set traps?

In the summer, the oceanside. In the spring a camp next to the waterfall, where there are weirs to net the alewives. There is feasting and dancing for everyone. In the fall and winter the bands break up; they will be hunters and follow the game into the woods.

Now it was dark. We were traveling through the woods. So many of us slipping among the trees, our feet on the matted underbrush, our hands held up in front of our faces to protect our eyes. And with all these hundreds, these thousands of feet, no sound except maybe a twig snapping. Not even that.
Overhead, the sky with the same stars.

Not far away there was a deserted camp—at the edge of the sea by the sandpit—with its blackened fireholes, paths that were trodden between the tents, piles of garbage, fish heads, cracked bones, and oyster shells. If I were to remember it.

But the dogs and the fleas were still with us.

At the same time I could hear there was traffic on the highway. There was a lighthouse on the high bluff. While the seagulls were asleep, it was sweeping the sea with its cold beam.

She was walking beside me carrying her house on her head, made of woven reed mats. She was so close I could feel her breath. I also thought, if I turned to her to speak . . . if I reached out and touched her, I'd lose her.
I thought: then I could weep for everyone.

All of us were moving through the woods of pitch pine. The animals fanning out ahead of us in panic flight, as before the smoke of a forest fire. Or perhaps we were following the animals.

Floating through the woods, over our heads a nighthawk or an owl coasting on its wings silently, magically, not even touching the branches.

Following the ghosts of animals. Or perhaps all of us dissolved, lifted, carried along by the fog rolling in from the sea.

We were all of us drifting uphill in the fog. Behind us the same sea, where the seagulls were sleeping. In the tidal flats, oyster beds. Walking on an earth without property lines.

The sea wind blowing at our backs. Following the ghosts of birds and animals.

Ghosts following ghosts.

Pushed by the wind. Without weight and in the silence like that of snow falling. On the dunes, on the ocean waves.

So many of us drifting. Waves upon waves of us. Up through the woods, through the darkness.

At the top of the hill there is a lighted house. We won't pass around it. We'll move through it.

■ Protecting Mendez

1

We've taken it upon ourselves to worry about Francisco Mendez's death. We wish to stop it. We don't want to learn who he is through his death.

There was always some mystery about Mendez. This may be just our own ignorance. We're unlettered rubber tappers; our horizon is limited. On certain higher levels there are people who know all about him, who understand everything and who anticipate everything. But this doesn't include the anticipation of his death.

In one way we know Chico absolutely. We work with him every day; you could say we share bread. There are others who are at a distance, who operate on a more abstract plane, who therefore tend to ignore certain things: for instance that there are people here who have it in for him, that assassins may be hired out from the local *cantina* for a few pesos. But because of these abstractions they're able to understand who Mendez really is.

He's wearing his wool poncho. It's still somewhat wet from the rain and therefore heavy. He's staring at the fire. And we also are wearing our wool ponchos and staring at the fire. The rain is pouring down in solid sheets, thundering on the tin roof. In the tropics there are twenty different kinds of torrential rain.

In the middle of the silence he has already moved away from us. He has been claimed by men in business suits who carry the Amazon in their briefcases.

We're tired and hungry. It's been raining for months. When it's absolutely hopeless, Mendez says, "I heard the other day they want to preserve the rain forest. Help is on its way."

We ask, "From where?"

"From a consortium of bankers. Or from certain quarters in Scandinavia."

Looking up toward the sky, into the immense roof of leaves, we expect to see angels coming.

This phrase: Save the Amazon rain forest, has been put into their ear by Mendez. But it also increases the chance of his death.

How do you make rubber? You score the tree diagonally with a knife, the incisions coming down to a point, catch the latex in a cup. These are all collected. Then you thicken the latex in an evaporator pan. The weight of the ball determines what you are paid. The plantation manager keeps the accounts. You have wages coming to you as a tapper. You also have an account at the store for what you buy.

This is what Francisco does. Like the rest of us, he's been a rubber tapper since the age of eight. At eighteen someone taught him to read, a soldier hiding out in the woods. Mendez taught us how to keep accounts, how to keep the owners, the *seringalistas*, from cheating us. Also we didn't go to the owners with our latex; we sold direct to the middlemen, the *marreteiros*. Or rather, we could do this. We did it and we could do it, when the price wasn't right.

We began keeping our own accounts. To the knowledge of how to tap rubber, the geometry of lines and incisions, and the chemistry of evaporation, we added the science of bookkeeping. That's not to say we were starving before and after that we were well off, that we lived in luxury, ate duck, and bought shoes of cordoban leather for our children. But we starved less. The few cruzos made the difference between living and starving.

Rain comes down. We look out from the clearing into the leaves, into thick jungle. We tell him, "There's danger out there. We heard them talking in town. The rubber barons, maybe some of the ranchers have put the word out. There could be an ambush."

Mendez laughs. "I've been ambushed six times. Each time I've escaped."

"Yes. But a man can't be lucky forever."

"Listen, we're in this. This fight isn't going to be won by corpses."

It's an old story. Chico Mendez is head of our rubber tappers union. Before him the union heads were threatened. In fact, all of them have been killed. And so will be the one who succeeds Mendez.

Still, he's confident. He's in the best of spirits.

The fires. In your nose and eyes, acrid smoke. It suits them, the ranchers, to clear the land. Beef cattle. Also the timber companies. Everywhere you look you see trees burning. These fires are not a few sticks under a pot, they're conflagrations. The logs pushed into a heap by the bulldozers. In the center there's a furnace of burning logs. You could walk in between them like a house. Timbers burning, falling, collapsing with a roar. It's not something you want to get close to. From the pile, smoke pours out red, purple, black into the sky.

This is what Mendez sees from high up. He sees all these fires. Not just one but hundreds. From Acre to Mato Grosso do Sul the whole Amazon is burning. This is what he sees from the window of the airplane. It hurts him. It makes him cry.

It may be this smoke drifts as far away as Sweden—certainly as far as North America—and will save the forest. Anyway, this is the message that Francisco brings when he goes to those meetings. He tells them, you sympathize. You care about us. But the powers in Brazil don't care.

There are others outside of Brazil who know who he is, but we don't know. We know Mendez, that's clear enough, because we rub shoulders with him. Even Mendez, who taught us how to read, this Mendez we're familiar with. After all, any person can learn. And a rubber tapper, even the poorest and most ignorant of us, has to be smart to get the better of the seringalistas. But to go beyond this and elevate it to some kind of principle—this is what we don't see.

Still, one shouldn't push one's smartness too far. What you're up against is the cruelty of the jungle.

The poor rubber tapper, dissatisfied with the price, gathers up his *princípio* to take to the marrietero. The princípio is his bundle of rubber wrapped in a parcel tied with the stray ends of rubber, the rubber strands. Going down the path, he is caught. The agents of the seringalistas catch him, tie him up by the strands of his princípio and burn him. What is this but cruelty? But it's perfectly logical on the part of the rubber owner. He has the power, so why not do it?

There are the flames. There is a circle of children watching. They have heard the screams and come running from the cabins of the rubber tappers or from an Indian village. And now the man is burning, the assassins are running away, the birds are crying overhead. Now there is just a little bunch of bones like sticks, a ring of black liquid and flames licking at the edge. The lesson.

As children we are watching. Chico as a child is watching with us. What we are absorbing is a kind of logic. It is the logic of the owner of the rubber trees, of the man who sells rubber.

Still, it's necessary not to starve. To counter this we have to be smart. The solution for us is never to go down the path alone, to always go in a group, all the rubber tappers together. In this way, the men waiting in the leaves can't do anything. They're outmaneuvered for a time. But only for this time. Because they own the trees. They own them or someone else owns them.

After the literacy episode when Francisco taught us to do our accounts and to bargain with the rubber barons, then he was wise enough to disappear. He hid out in the woods for a couple of years. But then he came out of hiding. He was with us working around the pans evaporating the latex. One day we were walking down the main street; we turned the corner into a side street, a dirt lane. And who did we run into but the cops beating up Francisco. His bag of groceries was strewn all over. His hat was lying in the dirt. One cop had him from behind by the arms, and two others were kicking him from the front, and clubbing him with their sticks. Chico was whooping and hollering. He's short and round with a barrel chest and mustache like an old fashioned barber. In a way the sight was comical. He was yelling, "Help! Murder! Assassins!" These were all guys he'd known from Xapuri. Every once in a while he'd say, "Hey, you guys are smart. You go right for a man's balls—like a real Portuguese." Sometimes he'd say, "I know they put you up to this. This is hurting you worse than me."

He'd walk away. Then he'd tell us later, "Look, they know me. I'm like them. If I were an Indian, they'd kill me."

But that was only the first. Since then there have been a thousand beatings. He is arrested, beaten, and tortured. His destiny is to survive beatings.

To live in the jungle requires trees. It never occurred to us that the jungle could go. It had always been there. But now they were cutting it down for the ranchers, and for the highway.

This success with the cops must have given him the idea for the *empate*. Maybe it wasn't Chico who invented it; we'd all thought of it. But he suggested it as something we could do.

The woodcutters arrive. They're in the clearing. All the equipment is there, the bulldozers, piles of logs burning, the roar of machines. They're cutting down the trees. At the same time the rubber tappers are there with their families, women and children, to implore them not to do it. This is called an empate. To show sympathy. What you're doing is showing sympathy for the woodcutters for having to saw down the trees. So there's a man sawing. We're all in the clearing, half-naked, both white rubber tappers and Indian. Around each tree there's a ring of us standing. Most of us are scared speechless. Even among those who are calling, the noise of the saws almost drowns us out. We're telling them, "Please. Don't you see what you're doing! Take your saws and go home."

We're astonished that our empate worked—that just by ringing the trees, and holding hands and weeping, we were able to plead with the loggers to go home. Not that they have gone home. Actually they went to another part of the forest, another place where they can cut down trees.

There are a thousand deaths in the Brazilian Amazon. This one would be special. Because of his bravery it would be a particular color, red, like a small orchid in the immense grey green of the rain forest. But the forest wouldn't know about it. But does the forest know any of us while we're alive?

We wonder at times who these people are. We don't know. But somehow or other Francisco must have contacted them.

There is a telephone here in Xapuri, though it's seldom used. Nothing ever happens around here. Besides, none of us has the money. So it must be for long distance. Conceivably any one of us could place a call to anywhere and to anyone, to some powerful person, the governor of a province or a bishop. And probably that's what happened with Francisco. He called them to tell them about the rain forest and about what's happening in the interior of the Amazon. After all, it's their rain forest, it's their Amazon Basin. They must care for it as much as we do.

The good thing about a rubber tree is that, if you use it correctly, no matter how many times you make the incisions—there can be dozens, scores running up the trunk—no matter how many times you tap it, if you let it rest a few months, a year, it will heal itself, it will go on giving rubber. Through the tapper's lifetime, the tree and the tapper's family will grow together. For our village to support itself, a few acres is enough. We don't need more.

One day we were sitting around with Chico. We had finished our daily labors and were resting. A child was drawing a ring in the mud with her toe. Chico was watching her.

Suddenly he said, "I've been talking to some officials, a lot of smart lawyers from Sao Paulo. What this should be is an Extractive Reserve."

We asked him, what did he mean?

At our question he simply shrugged, as if the answer were obvious. He said, lifting his cap and scratching his head,

"We just sit here. The word 'extractive' means it's used to get rubber. And the word 'reserve' means that it's reserved for us. We're allowed to be here."

We asked him why this was such a bright idea, since that's what we were doing now. And they were still cheating us.

"No. The difference is the law. It would be the law that we would stay here."

Now there is what is called "land fever," or the "Amazon fever." We, the rubber tappers, are only squatters. The ranchers can claim the land by clearing it, and this they can do by burning the trees . . . and by burning our crops and shooting at us.

The trouble was that for our next empate we had the bad luck to have chosen land belonging to the Alves brothers. Or so they claim to the land agency, the INCRA, that they own it. It is land they want to clear for a cattle ranch. A million acres.

What does that amount of land mean to us? We're only interested in a few trees. Size means nothing to us. Looked at from the Alves's side, it's different. For them it was a million acres of their own land. And Francisco was standing on it.

So we had this empate. We came there. At the same time, we had a demonstration at the offices of INCRA. In the grove of rubber trees, beside the chain saw operators, there were thugs hired by the Alves. There was violence. When we called out to the cutters to stop, shots were fired. Two of the rubber tappers were wounded.

2

Before, there were the seringalistas. But now with a fall in the world price for rubber, they are fewer. The rubber tappers are still here. We can survive because our expenses are less; we have the talent for starving. Why shouldn't the squatters—who are after all Amazonians and Brazilians—also become owners?

We know these ranchers—as well as we know the old seringalista agents—like the backs of our hands. They are like cousins to us. We see them; they ride around town every day in their jeeps. They are part of the town's power, and we are part of the town's powerlessness.

You could say that before our successful empate, the jungle was a simple place—just mosquitoes and rubber trees. Now there's the same amount of mosquitoes, but it's gotten to be visited by more people. Now Chico is known. Before he was indistinguishable from the rest of us, like the forest leaves.

At first they would arrive at the dock at Xapuri; they would ask us where this clearing is in the forest where they tap rubber and where they had this empate. "We've heard about it. How do you get there?" And they ask after Mendez, "What does he look like? Is he tall or short? How will we be able to recognize him?" Immediately they proceed to the clearing where we are working. When they see him, they'll ask him to give a speech, a statement on how the rain forest must be saved . . . and he obliges them, standing on a stump. Or they may forget they have come to see Chico. Once there, they may not even want to talk about the business at hand, so taken are they with the trees, and with the process of tapping rubber. It's as if they had never seen a tree. Or the photographers as if they had never seen an Indian. They seek out the poorest and most undernourished of the rubber tappers. Really they select our worst specimens. They are even disappointed that Francisco isn't an Indian, that he looks Portuguese.

Then there are the scientists, the ecologists, the naturalists, with their measuring tools. These measure the trees' size, the depth of the soil. They tell us how long the forest will last if it is undisturbed, how much it is going to rain. But we know how much it is going to rain. It will rain completely. Is this not the rain forest?

What we're telling Chico is that the whole thing, this adventure of the rain forest, has escalated. As for our plan, we hadn't thought ahead much. Everything had been done defensively. The trouble was, with each step, there was the perception that our plan was offensive. Not just against the ranchers and lumber interest, but now against the road builders. That we were moving forward. Like an army of soldier ants, we sought to devour everything. So we had triumphed over our enemies. But we had not wished to make enemies.

And had we actually improved the chances of the rain forest? Our campaign had secured a small piece of it for ourselves. But had we stopped the rest of it from being sawed down? Hadn't we in fact stimulated the sawing?

We were pointing this all out to Mendez. More was at stake now. Everything was on a different scale. And now the ranchers had their own viligante organization, the U.D.R., the *Uniao Democratico Rurale*.

He asked, "So what do you want?"—frowning at us. It's difficult to talk to Mendez.

"To be back where we were before," we told him. "It would have been better."

"You mean, if we'd done nothing?"

"Exactly. We wouldn't have all these worries."

"If we had done nothing, we wouldn't even be sitting here talking. We'd already be buried. The earth of the jungle would cover us."

The Amazon's a huge place. It goes on forever. For us it doesn't begin or stop. Xapuri is just a town on a river bank. When we look down it to where the river's going, perhaps it leads out of the rain forest to the sea. The river—when we look up to where it's coming from—leads perhaps to the mountains, to the cordillera. There is always the rain forest, just as there is always rain.

It is impossible to imagine that this rain forest has limits, just as it's impossible to imagine its being cleared. We hear from other Indians that this has happened. There are Indians and other tappers who have arrived here; they've fled from other places, and their villages in the bush are now cattle ranches, or they have been paved over for a highway. It's hard to believe them. Perhaps this is an exaggeration. But we ask ourselves, if it's still the forest and if they are lying, why would they be here?

To us who live in the jungle, it's simply what it is. What exists outside we don't know about or care about. Our first experience is noise. There is a continual droning of insects, screaming of birds, shrieking, chattering, and guffawing of monkeys. None of these can be seen. The source is hidden behind a wall of leaves. We also are inside the wall. Nothing ever cools the jungle; you are in a continual bath of moist heat, like steam.

In the jungle only the hunted and the hunting are silent. There is the heat and noise of the jungle—and a mysterious kind of light. It doesn't seem to come from the sky—a mysterious constant, unwavering green light, eaten by leaves. The jungle leaves, large to begin with, enlarge themselves to absorb this light, as they gorge themselves on the steam. For us there's the heat, the wet, the light emanating from the green leaves, the leeches. The ranchers. The snakes. The seringalistas. All these we have grown used to.

Now there are as many jeep tracks in the rain forest as there are alligator tracks. They sink deeper in the mud. But a jeep can navigate them. The roar of gas engines for generators is louder than the screaming of toucans, parakeets, macaws. Still—in comparison to the mass of the forest itself—these jeep tracks in the mud, these logging roads . . . even the rivers approaching Xapuri . . . are like spiders' threads, like the frailest tendrils of vines.

3

Mendez is just back from flying to one of his meetings. "They want to help us in Brazilia. This smoke, going up into the sky from all those fires, is beginning to get to them. And they're beginning to realize the bad effects of the highway."

He comes back from these meetings in certain cities in other parts of Brazil, or in certain foreign countries. When he gets back he is beaten—either by the local cops who don't think well of him; they have known him from the old days, he's just an ignorant laborer—or by the gang of thugs paid by these ranchers who have the land fever. When he returns to Xapuri, he is arrested and beaten—sometimes even worse.

We ask him: "Chico, is it worth it? Is it worth the pain? Here you've spoken to some important people in Brazilia, in Sao Paulo . . . to lawyers, to congressional representatives. And now you're lying in the dirt in Xapuri spitting out teeth."

"These ranchers are small-time players." He even jokes about the beatings. "These blows are hardly more than mosquito bites."

Chico is not different from us, only more talkative. It's as if he gave the trees a voice. Maybe this has been the real consequence of our empate. We ringed the trees, we pleaded with the chain saw operators, appealed to them with our tears, our rags, maybe even our smell of poverty. But our voices carried over their heads, out of the Amazon Valley to distant cities, Brazilia, Sao Paulo. Was it our fault that our message—which began simply with women crying—became a general message? That it was taken up by various groups, the labor unions, refugees from the drought in the Noreste, the church with its "opening to the poor," politicians, environmentalists? It became a national and patriotic message. The Amazon was Brazil. Where would Brazil be without its rain forest? What would the Amazon be without its forest cover? Like a woman shaved between the legs.

Also to the priests. With the loss of the trees, the church is seeing a loss of its congregation. After all, there must be Christians. You can't offer the sacrament to beef cattle.

You could say, these were all the people Mendez has been telephoning—not that it happened in exactly this way—and that he reached them all at once. Or that he knew with the first telephone call there would be a second, and where the whole thing was going. It was not enough to organize the forest; he had to appeal for help from the world as well.

He would make these calls at night, from the phone booth on the town square. We see him as we walk past. We come around the corner and there he is with the telephone to his ear. He's talking, smoking one cigarette after another. As we pass by he ignores us. Is he snubbing us? Or perhaps he doesn't notice us? There is a distant look in his eyes, directed away from us, to the person he is telephoning. Who is he telephoning? He stands in the lighted booth alone, with his back to the dark alleys and buildings. And beyond that the jungle.

We tell him, "Chico. Why stand out here in the light, where they can shoot you without even setting up an ambush? Here you're like a fish in a glass bowl."

We take our stand among the shadows to protect him. This has to be done discreetly. Francisco is proud. Or perhaps he enjoys the risk. He doesn't know we are guarding him. In the shadows we are unseen both by Chico and those who are stalking him.

People ask, how did Mendez organize the forest: consisting of 140,000 families of rubber tappers and countless Indians? To us the question is as wonderful as the accomplishment itself. It's true the rain forest is huge. But the settlements are closely linked, one just down the path from another. A jungle is not inhabited by solitary people—to survive in solitude is impossible. We are sociable. The Portuguese have their fiestas, their Sunday mass in the open air where they take a little wafer. The Indians have their tribal ceremonies. Chico simply went from one clearing to another—he is a fast walker—talked to them, they listened. He didn't even need to talk to them. The news of the success of our empate, and the idea of the extractive reserve where the forest would be ours traveled ahead of him. It illuminated the clearing like a sunburst, like the flashing wings of birds.

You could say the forest was not organized by Francisco, it organized itself. Under the threat of being empty, the forest encouraged its inhabitants to stay, to resist removal. This determination to stay has always been with us since the beginning, since latex was tapped. The coming of the rubber industry, which cheated us and starved us, only reinforced it. The rubber barons organized us to resist. Even though there was nothing to resist with except our own starvation.

4

Chico has a weakness for flying. Though he enjoys tapping rubber, he's good at it. He's one of our most skillful artisans. But then, too, he enjoys leaving the ground for the air. It may be these meetings excite him, the stimulation of talking to people in far-off countries.

It may be that these people are not so much charming Francisco as that he is charming them. "I was just speaking about the Indians the other day to a lady anthropologist in Brazilia, a charming woman . . . head of the Institute of Anthropological Studies . . . I was talking to a group of conservationists the other day about the jungle, about the beasts and birds."

We try to picture these people with Chico. "How do they treat you? Do they respect you?"

"Naturally, since they love the Amazon, they love Amazonians. There are a hundred different languages in the world. Not everybody speaks our dialect of Portuguese, or even *tacutu* Indian. At the meetings there are translations. So I could talk to them. They could listen to me for days. As for their being friendly, they take me to their homes—even the bankers. They offer me cigars, wine. As a mark of respect they even give me Portuguese sausage."

The word is out that Darli Alves murdered a man in the state of Paraná; he's a fugitive from there. He's here, claiming a million acres. Anyway, a warrant has been sworn out for his arrest. He's

in hiding on his estate, in the woods. He swears he will come out
and give himself up only after he has killed Mendez.

Not so long ago the journalists came to interview Chico, to get
the latest news about the Amazon and its tributaries and how
Chico has organized the Indians. Already they have lost interest
in what he has to say. They only want to listen to his voice; they
are content to snap pictures. His photo will appear in the news-
papers, or there's an item in the evening news on TV.

Usually our Indians do not paint their bodies when they are
working. This is reserved for artistic pleasure or for religious
ceremonies of different kinds, dancing and hunting. Once in a
magazine we saw Mendez talking with the president of some
province (it may have been some kind of protest). With him were
Indians in headdresses with as many feathers as a toucan and full
war paint. They were not Indians of our local tribe, or even our
portion of the Amazon, but from one of the other tributaries. It
doesn't matter how distant. There are many tributaries to the
Amazon and many tribes of Indians. For all, it's the same rain
forest.

One day we saw a photograph of Mendez talking to the presi-
dent of Brazil. (There was also a delegation of rubber tappers and
Indians.) And another of him talking to a group of bankers in
Mexico City.

"What did you say to them?" we asked him.

"I told Sarnoff to protect the Indians and not to listen to the
ranchers. The forest is bigger than they are. He won't listen. He
wants to build a highway going from Belém, at the mouth of the
Amazon, to the Andes."

"What did you tell the bankers?"

"These bankers are members of the InterAmerican Develop-
ment Bank. I told them not to lend money to Brazil to build the
highway, because they are destroying the rain forest. And they
also want to build a lot of hydroelectric dams in the forest. As if,
with all this rain, we don't see enough water. But I've got a bunch
of environmentalists working on this."

We asked him, "These people from so far away—why should
they care? If they are so far away from the Amazon, why do they
try to meddle with it?"

"It's true, they are less interested in the Indians than in the trees. They are not so interested in the trees as in what the trees do."

"What do they do?"

"It seems they produce something essential to air. They are responsible for the breathing of the whole world."

Later Francisco explains to us about the help that is coming.

"We're not in this world alone. There's more to the rain forest than Indians and rubber tappers."

That may be. But what we see here, nose to nose with us, are the rubber patrons and the ranchers. Why should we trust in friends whom we don't know and don't see, when we have to worry about an enemy that we rub up against, who makes us spit blood? We know what these ranchers dream about. Their sweetest dream—it is the dream of the Alves brothers—is that they are looking at the corpse of Mendez.

The rain forest is a huge place. In it the Indians and rubber tappers are small, like lice. But there are many of us.

They are beginning to hear our voices. The *federales*, government police, have been assigned to protect Mendez, to act as bodyguards. But who is to say they're not in the pay of the ranchers? And so we have to be even more vigilant.

5

Francisco returns. From the air he recognizes the country completely covered by forest as his own, the gleam of the river among the trees. He is already lost in the maze of the Amazon.

Flying over it he saw covering the whole landscape, fires. And pushing through the jungle, the highway. As if the promises made by everyone, by the distant powers he has been meeting with, amounted to nothing. The smoke of the fires and the wide swathe cut by the highway opposed to the jungle their own power. As if they are a prayer rising above the destruction. And have their own beauty and energy.

At the airport Mendez stands alone. Who is there on the ground to greet him?

But he has come back just to be our Mendez again. For this he must take off his shoes and put them in the traveling bag, change some bills, dollars into cruzos. He puts out his hand; it's raining, so he pulls on his poncho. He walks barefoot into the jungle.

But first, just to get acquainted, to see how the land lies, he takes a stroll through the town of Xapuri. He stops at the cantina for a drink. Later he tells us, "On the table there's this newspaper. A picture of me on the front page. I was having a drink of their best *grappa*—like mud. I had my nose in it discreetly. But this medal was hanging outside my shirt. Some of these bandits the Alves had hired were shooting darts and joking what a target I'd make.

"In Brussels they gave me this prize, from the World Conservation Society. They wanted me to stay and take it easy. But I told them I had to get back to Brazil. I had to tap rubber and harvest Brazil nuts to feed my family."

The flight back signifies a loss of respect. Mendez thinks, I was okay while I was flying above the earth. But now that my feet are on the ground, are the angels still with me?

To tap rubber is a dog's life and it hasn't gotten any better after the world has learned about us. In fact, the price of rubber has fallen, forcing us to work even faster. Everywhere you look there are rubber trees scored by knives. We've rescued the trees but perpetuated our own drudgery. The life of a rubber tapper is hurrying from tree to tree collecting these little cups, carrying them to the evaporator, carrying the little balls to the marrietero in the steaming heat. All this is done on the run with no let-up.

No let-up for Chico. He continues to work with us. His wife too, Elsamar. The eldest child stays home to care for the younger ones, or sometimes the whole family is there with Chico. Sometimes they work at night. This is not the only family to collect latex in the dark, the woman with a flashlight strapped to her forehead, the man lifting the pails. You'll see the whole of the forest alive with moving lights, like fireflies. The darkness of the night forest doesn't prevent us from being bathed in sweat.

Chico is still cheerful. In a way he's more cheerful than before.

"Look," Francisco tells us, "I'm in the business of tapping rubber. How else am I going to feed my family? Hunger doesn't go away by itself."

And he says, "I don't plan to die. But if I do die, don't have them put flowers on my grave. They'd be stolen from the Amazon."

It seems that our struggle and the images of our struggle grow independently of us—or even of Mendez. He may have started it, but long ago the process moved away from him. Not only pictures but songs. Very often you will see the Indians and Mendez talking with some official. The next day a song is made of it. They are accompanied by a band, one of our Brazilian bands. So that everywhere in Brazil there are songs and music accompanying our struggle to save the rain forest and the disappearance of the rain forest. It disappears and is saved. Mendez has become the symbol of its being saved and of its disappearance.

This is a symbol which we do not choose to interpret. Maybe they can interpret it. But for us, it is not the same Mendez.

The songs might make him popular throughout the whole Amazon, but they will make him more hated here in this part. That is, the songs help only where there are no ranchers, and where there is no pain from the Alves brothers.

The news of Francisco's arrival arrived before him. The newspapers tell us what he is thinking. He's working beside us; the news accounts, the stories, and the songs tell us what he is feeling—even how his muscles ache, how tired he is. Lifting the pail off the tree, we don't have to look at Mendez's face to know his sleeplessness. The sweat is pouring off his back.

This is not the same sweat, the same sleeplessness as with our Mendez. Naturally, these images won't die. They are composed of something other than flesh and blood. They are like mist that will always float over the Amazon.

The best protection for him is to make him just like the rest of us, indistinguishable from the forest leaves. We would like to hide him in the rain forest. Don't all rubber trees look alike? In the obscurity of this forest, he's just another rubber tapper. All he has to do is strip off his shirt and his shoes.

What it comes down to is, we are his protection. The rubber tappers, his own family and barrio. The circle of Indians. If he's a target in the village, it would be difficult to shoot at him; there are so many people around. That's not counting the guards.

The worst case is when he's alone. His cottage is at the edge of the clearing. There it's open; there's a few large *ceiba* trees. Space. When it's not raining, the sunlight comes in. But behind there's an outhouse. For modesty's sake, this is inside the woods. To reach it he uses the path. It could be . . . if he were to go there . . .

This could be what the Alves have been waiting for, Darli or Darcy Alves. They could follow him and finish him off that way. Or they would be hidden behind the leaves, waiting, and shoot him without being seen.

Even the forest doesn't protect Mendez.

This is the moment we've been guarding against. We've been watching for it and worrying about it. This moment, exactly, we can never allow to happen.

To live outside the rain forest is inconceivable. Living in it may be impossible. We manage to do it by working in the rubber grove, going to Xapuri for groceries from time to time, by avoiding leeches. The same rain. The children with runny noses. The same work. The same poverty. The same anteaters. Is this the paradise—an "extractive reserve"—Mendez has been telling us about? If it is, it's a paradise where the world is collapsing around the edges. Around the edges there is the smell of smoke, the whine of chain saws.

What we're living in turns out to be a paradise only so long as we're not expelled from it.

It's raining. It's always raining. In the rain forest it steams and rains. The Amazon is a river of rain.

We look out from under the shelter where we evaporate the latex. In the downpour the cups attached to the trees have been protected with little hats.

Francisco is wearing only a pair of ragged shorts. He's slapping at mosquitoes. From its chain hangs the little medal. His body is covered with scars, lumps, bruises from the last ambushes and beatings.

He stretches his legs, scratches himself. He tells us, "These mosquitoes don't bite me. I'm made of cast iron."

In the trees, high in the canopy over our heads, even the parakeets and the monkeys have been muffled in the steam.

Looking up at them, Mendez tells us, "Help is coming."

Above the leaves, he can imagine himself traveling back and forth in a plane. He can imagine himself weeping.

We would like to persuade Mendez not to fly.

■ Six Ways of Looking at Farming

1

The Lalumieres were anticipating the auction with dread. The farm was to be auctioned—buildings and equipment. Here is a typical newspaper notice:

February Specials
> 316 acre dairy farm—155 tillage, 100 pasture, 220 x 36 comfort stall barn, 109 stalls, 20 x 70 and 20 x 50 concrete silos with unloaders, 110 milkers, 23 young stock, full line of modern equipment.
>> Stocked and equipped—$425,000
>> Bare—$350,000

The Lalumieres had seen such notices for a long time; only now it applied to them.

Let's not describe the auction itself. The household items are sold off: these have been collected and stored on the porch, and are sold for small amounts to random buyers who might take a fancy to such things—let's say, an old music box. Equipment: tractors, mower-conditioners, seed drills, balers, and silage choppers. These go to other farmers and equipment dealers. Then the herd itself . . . by now the crowd has moved inside the barn, glad to be out of the rain. A good holstein with calf in her going from $900 to $2,000. The land. Then finally the farmer's debt to the moneylender is paid off. The crowd has left. It's stopped raining. The family is sitting on the porch looking out at the empty yard where the flowers have been trampled, at the empty equipment bays, at the empty barn—but with enough cash to keep going.

It is the Lalumieres sitting here. The story has already taken us beyond the bare words of the auction notice: "February specials. 316 acre dairy farm . . . 155 tillage," into the zone of sadness. The family is sitting on the porch together. Each feels it in a different way. It's all over, the noisy theatricality of the public event. At their backs is the emptiness of rooms. A lilac bush crowds on the porch railing. It reaches out toward them . . . its blossoms still wet, deepened in scent and color, hanging in their weight.

2

Some months before, Ed and Therese Lalumiere were sitting at the kitchen table. The old man was in a characteristic pose for him—with his head down resting on his arms, fists pressed against the temples. He was short, his barrel chest pushed against the table edge, his arms like butcher blocks. Next to the fist, a pocket calculator. Therese stood behind him, her back to the refrigerator, half an ear toward the grandson napping upstairs, glad that his volcanic energies were for the moment sleeping.

The financial papers were spread on the family dinner table— account books, copies of tax forms, paid bills, bank statements, etc. Sheets in piles clipped together covered the surface as solidly as plates.

This is what they amounted to:

EXPENSES: Food and household expenses, transportation, utilities, phone, medical.

Grain, herbicide, fertilizer. Equipment maintenance. Insurance, veterinary, seed.

Taxes. Repayment of loan.

INCOME: Twice-monthly milk check. Logging. Trailer rental.

Market value of farm listed—40% of equity in loans.
Overall zero or minus income.

The point was: there was no way out.

No need to think about it. No need for the two to speak to each other of blame, failure, of fortitude, resilience, of cunning calculation, of hope. This is what the figures added up to. They had been gone over a thousand times.

The old man's pose—short stocky frame, head resting on arms, fists to the temples, etc.—not of despair but simply the posture of a man with emphysema. A way to relax the tension of the neck and give some room for breathing to the lungs.

The point was, there was no way out. No matter which way one moved, nothing would give an inch—as if the landscape: trees, fields, every blade of grass were made of iron.

Therese with her back to the refrigerator, looking out the window at the big maple, from whose limb was suspended by a chain a car engine.

Business of the farm continuing as usual. The daughter-in-law in town working. The son—repairer of the engine—now in the barn milking eighty cows. And the grandmother looking after the grandson.

She's listening for his waking, ear tuned to his stirring and shouting, his step stamping downstairs. Already she feels his hand inside hers pulling and tugging this way and that in childish circles, dragging her—the willing captive—on one errand or another.

3

One day the farmer had passed a group of Haitians picking apples in his neighbor's orchard. The men worked speedily on ladders, arms reaching upward through the leaves, twisting, dropping the fruit into bags tied to them. The gang moved down a row of trees stripping them of fruit.

Later Ed Lalumiere was able to observe two of these imported laborers in the supermarket. The language, of course, was incomprehensible to him. What struck him most was their shirts: blue, faded, worn through and many times mended. In the aisle, sheltered by the walls of canned goods, they chattered volubly. But they became silent and guarded. And going through the checkout counter, they couldn't answer questions but stared dumbly.

As Lalumiere passed by the orchard, one picker—a man the same age as himself—was standing by the fence pissing. The

Haitian, who had his front teeth missing, was only a few feet from him.

Behind him the gang of apple pickers performed their task in the orchard aisles among the trees. They worked rapidly, chattering among themselves with a raucous and surreptitious air. They were like a flock of crows.

The squad of laborers, imported by the Immigration Service, came from overseas. They lived in dormitories and were all men. The pickers, who were all bone and sinew, who could work all day in the air without stopping . . . whose hands were coal black and whose eyes were slightly bloodshot . . . seemed to Lalumiere immeasurably strange.

4

Therese had read a story about a farm in the west. It was foreclosed and about to be sold at auction, and the neighbors prevented bids from being taken. It was unclear whether their farmer-neighbors had guns. The farm was being auctioned off at the instigation of the bank. Undoubtedly there were buyers, but due to the feeling of solidarity among the crowd of farmers, their sense that what was happening was unfair and wrong, it was not possible for the auctioneer to begin.

There were a number of conceivable happy endings to the story. But simply reading the story—that such a thing should happen—gave Therese joy. She had showed the item to Ed—who was tickled.

This item of news contrasted to her own nightmare. She had dreamed they were having an auction. It was their farm that was being sold off by the local auctioneer, a man named Pratt. Everyone knew Pratt. A jovial man, he had relatives in town. For years they had gone to Pratt to buy and sell cows. But in the dream he was wearing a frock coat.

Pratt was speaking in a strange language, or his patter was unusually garbled. Though it seemed he was speaking to her, she couldn't understand a word of it. One of the townspeople explained that he was saying this auction was special, it would be held under a unique set of rules. There was of course a money price on the farm, corresponding to what was bid. But also the work done on the farm by the Lalumieres would count; that is, it could be reckoned in a dollar figure—the years the family had spent living there for four generations and the value of the farm to the town: its beauty, its open fields and woods. For all these, the Lalumieres would receive a cash credit.

"But these things—everything we put into it—don't count," Therese objected. "It don't work out that way."

"It's true, they have only a symbolic value," the neighbor told her. "But so has money only a symbolic value." She assured her that the townspeople would stand as witnesses for the Lalumieres. And so they would be able to enter the bidding.

She had been told that the prospective buyer of the farm was there, or the buyer's agent. Therese looked for him but couldn't find him. She kept looking for this person, whom she imagined as a foreigner, some hostile power. Somewhere there must be this baleful figure.

The bidding began, but the unknown buyer had not materialized. Instead, Therese realized, it was the neighbors themselves who were bidding against her. As in all auctions, bids were made by signs, a nod of the head or the flick of an eye, traced by the auctioneer. She was scanning the faces. The audience remained more or less expressionless, the eye of the auctioneer merely traveling over them as his lips moved, traversing the faces and picking up the secret signs.

The bidding had begun. The townspeople and neighbors were all familiar. It was all ordinary. That's what made the dream more terrifying.

5

As he drove the tractor, Jack Lalumiere could turn his head and watch the baler, pulled by the tractor, extrude the bales of hay onto the large flatbed wagon, which was pulled behind that. On the bed, a farmhand caught the bales as they came off and swung them onto a pile in back.

The helper was a Vietnamese or Thai laborer, a man twice the age of Jack. He was agile. Due to his short stature, the man had difficulty piling the bales. He had to stand on his toes to reach the top, to position them on the structure which was slightly quaking.

At the barn, when the wagon load was full, the bales of hay would be lifted by conveyor to the second-story loft.

There were woodchuck holes in the field. Where it had been cut, the field showed a mat of brownish white against the uncut green. With the large tractor and rig two men could harvest thirty acres of hay in a day in the June heat.

The tractor's path, parallel to the hedgerow, continued in a straight line in slow motion through the grass. It was as if it were a ship: Jack at the wheel was the pilot, and the farm laborer—with his wispy patriarch's beard and rope sandals, feet spread and bracing himself—was a deckhand . . . moving through seas of green.

Jack rarely looked back. The laborer concentrated on his task. The driver's attention was on the window, the swathe of hay being taken up by the machine, in front of which swarms of grasshoppers were flying up and moving out to the sides in silent waves. The tractor puttered along dreamily.

A flock of crows lifted from the field, circled, cawing and scolding, and disappeared over the wood. The wood seemed to be the true kingdom of the crows.

The hedgerow extended the length of the field. It had once been a line of fence but had grown up to shrubs—alder and buckthorn, and more substantial trees—so that it was now a dense barrier, a bulwark of impassable shadow. Beyond it could have been woods or wilderness. In fact, at the bottom could be seen chinks of light, crossed by an occasional strand of barbed wire. The openings could have been made by some animal browsing there. Jack remembered it as once being a pasture with cow-plop and purple thistles. There had been a gate somewhere. Several years ago he had looked for this entry point but had failed to find it. Jack remembered they used to go through the fence somewhere. That was long ago. They had walked through the field, he and the neighbors' children, with their bathing suits, and at the bottom there was a river and pools. After swimming they would lie on their backs on their towels, arms behind their heads, looking up at the sky.

That time was far away, forever inaccessible. What was barred by the impassable hedge was not so much a place, but a time. It was the territory of childhood.

6

The three men were bathing in the pool. The river entered after a stretch of rocky shallows, and left the place over a lateral shoulder of rock the water had smoothed. The river made a long curve around the hay field, forming several pools. The deepest and coolest was this spot where the men were bathing, splashing the water with their arms or buoyed up and half floating, balancing on the bottom with their toes.

Ed Lalumiere's body was the most compact, like a block of wood. The Vietnamese, also short, was thinner and frailer, his skin paler in the moonlight. The Haitian floated on his back half submerged like a black tree that had fallen in and the current was carrying along.

The bathers' pool insisted on its own quiet. It was night. And perhaps the flowing water did their speaking for them. Or it was enough for the moonlight to tell a plain story written on the newly mown hay field, which glowed like a piece of paper. The alfalfa stems gave the field a stippled effect.

The moon didn't seek out the church steeple or any number of metal roofs of houses. Or if it did seek them out they were merely points of light glancing off the sleeping town.

At some point in the night bathing the West Indian, who was tall and rangy, would have clambered up on the stony lip, his arms dripping, and edged his feet ahead warily so as not to slip, and bent down, like a heron fishing. Lalumiere may have sat back against the mud bank which rose vertically, his eyes open wide because in the night freshness he was able to expand his lungs fully. And the Vietnamese farmer would have simply floated, hardly moving, his head tilted back, like a petal, not so much submerged in the water, as in memory.

He had been soaping himself, rubbing the dust of the day's work and hay chaff off. He smelled sweet. So perhaps it was a woman's body he was remembering.

All of the men submerged in memories. Or they were floating

above their memories hardly conscious of them. They had drift-
ed down, sunk below the illuminated surface, into the dark. They
were no longer bitter or sweet memories, light or dark, but con-
fused sediment at the bottom, and the bathers were swimming
over them.

If it had been daylight, the three would have been stretched
out on top of the bank sunning themselves. They would have
been talking with each other about soils, the merits of different
feeds, the cost of fertilizer and seed, what price a cow or goat
would fetch at the market. Of the tricks and dodges of bankers
and moneylenders. Of how farms could be lost through debt.

They could have talked about all of this as they lay drying on
the banks. If the glare of the sun behind the eyelids had not been
too red. Or the sky had not been too blue. Or the sun's heat
reaching through their pores had not made them too sleepy.

But now it was night. They were swimming, disembodied in
the pool. It was moonlight. They had floated beyond the bank's
shadow.

They were refreshing themselves. The day's work was over.
The townspeople were in bed. The field was full of sleeping grass-
hoppers. The woods were owned by owls. The river, as it slipped
by, had its arm around the waist of the fields.

"Comme s'bon s'baigner," Lalumiere whispered, in a language
long since forgotten. It had been the language of his grandmoth-
er . . . which now came up into him through his toes. Good to
swim, to be floating in the cool water, to be refreshed, to be with
companions. "Comme s'bon s'baigner," Ed Lalumiere repeated,
thrashing with his arms and propelling himself forward in the
direction of the Haitian.

Who reared up at him laughing and repeating with a shout,
"Oui. C'est bon se baigner!" Recognizing it was his own language
but a different patois. He spouted water at Lalumiere through his
teeth.

"S'bon s'baigner. Comme t'dis," the Vietnamese murmured, his
eyes crinkled at the corners and sweeping his arms forward at
the pleasure of the strangeness being broken by words.

Designed by Martha Farlow

Composed by Blue Heron, Inc., in
Trump Medieval with Gill Sans Bold display

Printed by The Maple Press Company, Inc.,
on 55-lb. Glatfelter Antique Cream

This page constitutes a continuation of the copyright page.

Stories in this collection have appeared in the following periodicals: "The Secret Radio Station" in *Another Chicago Magazine*; "The Mirror of Narcissus" in *Minnesota Review*; "The Barn Raising" in *Mesechabe*; "The Changing Beast" in *River Valley Voice*; "The Warehouse" in *The Socialist Review*; "In the Air" in *Minnesota Review*; "The Hostage" in *Witness*; "Guatemala" in *Ikon*; and "Visitors to the Cape" in *Blatant Artifice*.